praise for

Hamburgers and Berliners
and other courses in between
by Matt Potter

Potter examines the differences between cultures big and small – between countries, continents or, at the other end of the scale, the microcultures that exist within a block or a street. He constantly questions the what and the why of things, observing idiosyncrasies and habits and ingrained patterns of thought in a way that makes you see your own surroundings and behaviours afresh. Never uncomfortably disrespectful (though often funny), Potter had me smirking with some of his descriptions and going "Aha!" at others.

~ Gill Hoffs, author of *The Sinking of RMS Tayleur: The Lost Story of the Victorian Titanic* and *Wild: a collection*

Matt Potter unflinchingly allows us inside his mind and heart, sharing fears and insecurities that most of us would never dare to reveal. His book is both poignant and funny, and through Potter's eyes we get a vivid picture of Germany – its landscapes, people, customs and quirks – while also witnessing one man's struggle to make sense of his own life as well as life at large.

~ Len Kuntz, author of *The Dark Sunshine* and *I'm Not Supposed to Be Here and Neither Are You* praise for

Based on True Stories
by Matt Potter

Matt Potter's writing voice possesses a delicate snark, an incisive wit that lifts even the commonplace into unique memorability. The characters who saunter — sometimes wander, sometimes traipse — throughout this collection of bite-sized fiction have the makings of great fictional people: they're singular and quirky, but somehow, at the same time — and here's where my admiration for Matt's skill goes off the chart — they're possessed of an indisputable sense of reality ... These people exist, they live and breathe, and we, the readers, recognize in them our friends, our family ... And ourselves.

~ Guilie Castillo Oriard, author of *The Miracle of Small Things* and *It's About the Dog*

The small fictions in *Based on True Stories* will not lull you — they will piss you off or, at the least, move you to indignation, or tears, or laughter. Maybe all three. These gems provoke, like the tip of a chef's knife pricking skin, and just as the words get uncomfortable, the story delivers the bit of redemption that reveals the humanity of his characters — and of us all. These stories are real, raw, and honest. The reading doesn't get much better than that.

~ Linda Simoni-Wastila, Senior Fiction Editor at *JMWW*

on

the

bitch

a summer novella

Matt POTTER

TRUTH SERUM PRESS

TRUTH SERUM PRESS

On the Bitch copyright © Matt Potter
First published as a book February 2018 by Truth Serum Press

ISBN: 978-1-925536-45-4

Truth Serum Press
32 Meredith Street
Sefton Park   SA   5083
Australia

Email: truthserumpress@live.com.au
Website: http://truthserumpress.net
Truth Serum Press catalogue: http://truthserumpress.net/catalogue/

Cover design by and cover photographs (both Horseshoe Bay, Port Elliot)
copyright © Matt Potter
Author photograph used by permission © Kathryn Garrett

Also available as an eBook
ISBN: 978-1-925536-46-1

Truth Serum Press is a member of the
Bequem Publishing collective
http://www.bequempublishing.com/

Also by Matt Potter

*Hamburgers and Berliners and
other courses in between*
(travel memoir)

Based on True Stories
(short stories)

Vestal Aversion
(short stories and short non-fiction)

*all you need is … a whiteboard, a marker
and this book!* (Book 1 and Book 2)
(ESL teacher resources)

for Gill

who wants to meet Magda

Contents

Friday

1   Carbon Footprint

4   What you see is what you get

6   Glass

8   Pile

11   Ein Ausflügler in Schwerin

14   The eyes have it

17   Indian

20   Scarf

23   Deluge

26   Samoa

Saturday

31   Morning

35   Sugar-whacked

40   Smoking Gun

43   Build

46   Kids

51   Broken

54   Schmutzig

57   Coffee

62   Am Gendarmenmarkt

66   In Memoriam

69   Dream

77   Cream

82   Zapped! again

89   Lights Out

Sunday

97   Communication is the key

100   Ming

106   Penguin

113   With a sea view

118   Hardware

125   The Apple of a Nun's Eye

128   Schokolade

131   Shiraz

134   Popular

142   Favour

146   Destination

150   Acknowledgements

151   Thanks

153   About the Author

Friday

Carbon Footprint

"Thank you for driving us, Otto," says Magda, light blue eyes earnest in her tanned face. "The environment will thank you, too."

I breathe in the new-car-leather smell and push my sunglasses to the bridge of my nose. Warm late summer air blasts through the open window. Shimmering street signs and trees – leaves edging yellow and brown – blur as we speed past.

We're hunched in the alcove (aka the back seat) of Otto's latest toy, a red BMW two-door soft-top. Magda's knees rest just under her chin. Our backpacks sit between us on the soft black leather and already my fifty-six year-old hips are begging for mercy. The ninety-minute trip to Otto's beach place – it's not a shack or even a house, more of a showcase from what he's told me – will wear out its welcome on our arses too.

Kendalynn turns in the front passenger seat and smiles at us. "We were coming past Stepney anyway."

The car – or Otto's foot on the accelerator? – throbs beneath us, threatening to blast off, the engine too powerful for its compact body. Ducking and weaving through the

2pm Friday traffic, I hope other drivers aren't thinking I share Otto's too-late-by-a-decade mid-life crisis.

"We had to buy some meat at the butcher up at Magill so we really *were* driving past." Kendalynn smiles wider. Her freckled face – surprisingly unlined for her mid-fifties – barely creases in worry but her eyes beg us to believe her. She looks at Otto behind the wheel. "Weren't we?"

The red BMW sails through traffic lights as we speed on.

Kendalynn's freckled hand reaches across and strokes Otto's hair just above his ear. "We thought we'd do a lamb roast in the barbecue." The rings on her fingers – pink rubies and a diamond cluster – glint in the light shining through the BMW's sunroof. (Yes, there's a sunroof in the soft-top!) And Otto's hair, once fiery red, is thinner and greyer than six months ago. "Didn't we?"

"Yeah," says Otto, powering past convent arches on the left and a Catholic boys' school on the right, "you can't beat a good roast."

I squirm on the seat. My bare arms are already sticking to the leather, my arse is already half-numb and my mind is already half-elsewhere.

"Remember those great roasts your mother used to make, Hugh?"

Not even out of the suburbs and he's reminiscing.

"Carrots and parsnips and potatoes and pumpkin. What was her secret?" Otto turns the steering wheel and nips into the next lane.

"Dripping," I say, hands rubbing the tops of my thighs. "Lamb fat. Lots of lamb fat. Giant vats of lamb fat. Collected in a metal bowl and reused after every meal."

"Who cooks lamb now?" Otto asks. "Banished and replaced by fucking mung beans and alfalfa." He flicks the steering wheel and changes lanes again.

"Mung beans and what?" asks Magda.

"Lamb was the meat everyone ate every day when we were kids." I sound like a social historian. And nod at my own wisdom.

"Twice a day," adds Otto. "Three times a day. *More* if you were on the land."

Magda screws up her nose. "Lamb is so *fatty*."

"Ah, you can't knock lamb, Magda," says Otto. "Australia was built on the sheep's back."

I slide in my seat again. In less than five minutes we'll be on the freeway heading through the Hills to the coast. And my hips and my calves and my thighs and my knees are screaming for a roadstop halfway.

"If everyone was eating so much lamb," Magda asks, "how much was left for building Australia?"

What you see is what you get

"People think I am crazy, but I was not crazy before I lived in this country," Magda says, throwing her sweaty-under-the-armpits t-shirt on the floor. She flips open her backpack, reaches in, and pulls out a full-steam iron.

"No one thinks you're crazy, Magda." I look through the guest room window, onto the street running behind the house. That's *our* view. Views of the beach are reserved for the non-guests, the people who actually own this pile of bricks and cement and glass, who actually pay for it.

"They think I am just a forty-nine-year-old crazy foreign woman," Magda says, "from Germany, who brings an iron with her when she goes to the beach for a holiday during the weekend."

She pulls out the small plastic jug she uses to fill the full-steam iron with water, and sets it beside the bedside lamp.

"But you know what would be really crazy?" she says. "And I have been living in Australia since two years so I know what people think is crazy."

"What?" I sit on the edge of the bed and unroll my right sock 'til it's under my heel. I grab it from the toe and pull. It springs off my foot and snaps against my fist.

Magda looks me in the eye as she reaches behind her back and unsnaps her bra. Her eyes are clear blue. "If I was also to bring an ironing board. So then I would be *really* the crazy foreign woman from Germany." She laughs. Her bra falls off into her hands. Her breasts are small and nut-brown.

I stand up and grabbing her 'round the waist, pull her towards me. Soon she is riding me, my own legs spread as I drive my cock into her, gasping with each thrust, a smile spreading across her face as her fingers pull at the grey hair curling on my chest.

And just as her eyes roll up, I hear, "Oh fuck."

I shoot a look over at the door cracked open.

"I mean, oh God," Otto says, fresh bathroom towels in his arms. "Sorry."

The door clicks shut.

Magda looks down at me beneath her, shrugs her shoulders, moves her hips. I groan and push into her.

A little later, she rolls off me, hair stuck to her forehead. She always works up quite a sweat when she comes.

I slide on the mattress to make space. Breathing together, we lie looking up at the whiter-than-white ceiling, listening to the sea rolling outside and sharing the dilemma: what do we say – or do we say anything – to Otto?

Magda sighs, and I taste her breath on my face as she whispers, "Now he can say I really am the crazy foreign woman from Germany, because I like to fuck with the iron next to the bed."

Glass

We stand on the balcony and watch her striding up the beach, blonde hair flying in the breeze, long legs high-stepping like a gazelle.

"Zap!" she says, pointing the wand at the sand and blasting it with a jolt of electricity. Then two steps forward and "Zap!" again.

"What's the crazy frau doing now?" Otto says, putting his glass on the balcony rail and shielding his eyes with his other hand. Otto invited us to stay for the weekend, but his generosity sometimes comes at a cost.

I look out across the sand again and see yes, of course it looks ridiculous. But what great idea doesn't look slightly odd to the uninitiated?

"She got it on the internet," I say. "It's called a Zapper. It zaps things."

Otto sips his gin and tonic – he's a big sipper – and with the sun behind him, looks at me like I'm a piece of seagull shit in the kiosk car park. "So you're gonna let her walk up and down the beach zapping things like some bag lady with a secret weapon?"

"I'll let you in on a secret," I add, my voice low. "Yes."

"Zap!" Magda says again on the beach. And then for emphasis, she gives two blasts of the wand. "Doppel zap!"

Otto shakes his head. "You can't afford to put petrol in your car to get here, but you're wasting money on shit you buy on the internet? Where's the forward thinking, Hughie?" And he stabs my forehead with his thumb.

"You just gotta have faith, Otto," I say, pulling away. His breath on my face smells gin-and-tonic-y. He's probably more of a glugger than a sipper. "She's got our future in her hands."

Otto sighs, and shakes his head again.

I smile the knowing smile of the smug, and lean over the balcony into the wind. "You're doing a great job, sweetie," I call out.

Funny, I've never called her "sweetie" before.

Magda turns, her concentration broken. And taking off her sunglasses, waves them in the direction of the house. Her windmilling arm unbalances her and she topples over, bent-over bottom facing the foreshore.

"Nice tail," Otto says. And turning to walk back inside his million-dollar shack, he adds, "And I thought the iron by the bed was weird."

Pile

"Who's gonna take on this pile when I'm gone?" Otto asks.

Otto stretches his arms wide, looking up at the sprawling beach house like he's begging forgiveness. We're standing barefoot on the lawn, the beach behind us, sun blazing through our t-shirts.

"We need to do something about this sand," Kendalynn says, her broom whisking across the wide front porch. "Otto, it's getting into the house."

Otto rolls his eyes, like he doesn't trust his wife's judgement, or he knows something she doesn't, or she really is the trophy wife who understands nothing.

"It's a beach house, love. On the beach. Where sand is a fact of life."

Kendalynn drags the broom to the edge of the tiles, just as the breeze blows more sand onto the porch. "Lucky it's not your job to sweep it up every day."

"Get someone in to do it." Otto's voice is raspy and fed-up. "Use your noggin', woman." He raps his knuckles against his skull, gold signet rings glinting in the sun.

"There are no Asians living on the South Coast, Otto, you *know* that."

"Yabber yabber yabber." Otto flaps his hand like a mouthy sock puppet.

Kendalynn stomps inside. The door slams.

I shift from one foot to the other. Have I slipped into their domestic reverie without them noticing? But no, we actually came outside because a neighbour in the next-door rent-a-holiday-palazzo — but do holiday-palazzi *have* neighbours? — said he saw an emu on Otto's roof.

"No ambition, my daughters," Otto says, stretching his arms out again like he can't believe his fortune, good and bad. "No interest in business. No sense of competition. No drive. Nothing! Now what am I gonna do with *this* place? Leave it to them to turn into a retreat for muff-munchers?"

Maybe this weekend at the beach is a mistake.

His eyes scan the façade, all glass and marble and metal and slate. Given emus can't fly, there is — naturally — *no* emu on the roof.

"Give it to charity," I say.

Pig's arse, his look says. Then shrugs his shoulders and hands on hips, shakes his head in wonder. "Magnificent." He whistles through his teeth, then steps back, standing behind me to get an even better view.

"And what about you, son?" Otto only calls me *son* when dispensing advice about love or career or money or politics or marriage or business or life. Even though we're the same age. "Going back to Germany again?"

I look out at the beach, Magda still zapping in the distance.

"I've got another twelve months on my contract here," I tell Otto. "And Magda's got her behavioural consultancy."

Otto looks at me. "Behavioural consultancy?" He shakes his head again and shrugs his shoulders again. "You're getting older, son."

"We haven't talked about it. Magda's living at my place. I still enjoy teaching. So I'm here for another twelve months."

Otto digs his big toe into the lawn. "Fuck, we're all getting older." Now he's nodding his head. "No, *you're* not getting much older, are you? That's 'cause you never had kids. Bloody lucky – they break your heart and fuck you over."

Kendalynn opens the door. "Valerie just rang on the mobile," she says. "She's coming down tomorrow. *Early.*" The door slams again.

Otto throws up his hands. "Christ, that'll be a corker start to the day!"

Ein Ausflügler in Schwerin

Going back to Germany again? Otto asked.

Meine Damen und Herren, the voice had announced over the loudspeaker, two years earlier. But my mind had switched off already, the half-empty train slowing into the Ludwigslust Bahnhof. Hands gripping headrests, people stood up to get off.

Sitting in the seat opposite, Magda's head nestled into the blue headrest, angled towards the window. Her face had relaxed as she slept, the lines around her eyes soft, wisps damp at her hairline, and her chest rose and fell with each breath in the humid carriage.

Across the aisle an older couple sat down, beside each other, facing the front (I faced the other way), a bag on both their laps.

Neck sticky against the headrest, eyes off to the side, I watched them.

The carriage doors sighed shut and the train pulled out of the station, white-on-blue *Ludwigslust Bhf* signs blurring as it sped up. The wife – both were grey-haired with thin, lined faces – opened the bag on her lap while her husband unlatched the tray table from behind the seat in front of him and eased it down.

She pulled a plastic container out of her bag – small and square with a pale blue lid – and opening it up, took out two bread rolls (*Schrippen* in Berlin), both wrapped in foodwrap. She handed one to her husband, then pulled down her own tray table. Each peeling off the plastic, they bit into them, the Schrippen yawning open and, as I expected, revealing cheese and slices of meat.

Such precision.

I watched, lying still in my seat, eyes half-closed in case they saw me and stared back.

They spoke to each other as they ate – I couldn't hear what but it didn't matter – and then halfway through their Schrippen, the wife dipped into her bag again and took out a *Ritter* chocolate bar. Then picked up her Schrippe and bit into it again.

The husband nodded at the chocolate, and said something small.

Grey hair short at the sides and fuller on top, camel sleeveless jackets and camel trousers, beige walking shoes and pinky-beige shirts: his thin-striped and hers small-flowered, so alike they were hard to separate. Perhaps they bought their lives in a job lot. And like many older German couples, wore identical expressions. (Lost in a crowd? Easy, just look for your twin.)

Passing trees on the flat north German plain played shadows through the window on Magda's sleeping face and I thought, no, I do not want to grow old in this country. At fifty-four years old (as I was then), I knew I did not want to look like an ageing cipher, beaten down by habit and expectation and timetables and grind. I watched the couple pass the chocolate between them. And turned away.

"What are you thinking?" Magda asked.

I breathed in, the cologne in my chest hair fragrant in the cloying warmth, and smiled. "About how much I'm looking forward to spending the day with you in Schwerin."

The eyes have it

"What do you feel like?" Kendalynn asks. Unsure if she means me (I'm walking to the kitchen for a glass of water), I step into the room.

The room is lined with shelves chockfull of dolls, so many it's hard to see where one over-dressed doll stops and the next over-stuffed nightmare starts. They all stare back at me. Up and down, left and right, backward and forward: wherever I move, their eyes follow me. There must be a hundred of them.

"Indian or Chinese?" says Kendalynn, sitting in a large floral armchair by the window, takeaway menus in her manicured hands. "Or" – she flips the third menu over – "Chinese-Indian."

"No lamb?"

"Otto wants to cook that tomorrow."

"You have a lot of dolls, Kendalynn."

"Otto hates them, so I have to keep them in here." She holds up the yellow and red and orange and blue and green menus. "Which one?"

"Indian," I say.

She opens the Indian.

"He won't even come into this room," she says. "So it's all mine." And she opens her arms wide, menu flapping in her hand, welcoming me to her hideaway.

I'm drawn to the dolls again. They all have a generic look, sandy hair and blue eyes and pale, freckled skin. Some are dressed in hats and many have glasses, all have china feet – some with cuts for toes and some with shoes – sticking out under frilly hems.

"I only ever had one doll when I was a girl so I've dressed all these dolls myself." Kendalynn rests her glasses on the end of her nose to read the menu. Then looks at me with her sandy hair, blue eyes and pale, freckled skin. "It's a hobby I wish I could pass onto Otto's daughters."

I picture Otto's lesbian separatist daughters swamped in frills and frou-frou.

Well, actually, I can't.

"I feel like something adventurous for dinner. Makkai camel curry with corn cobs," Kendalynn reads, the dolls' eyes watching us with hunger, or boredom, or both. "Do you think Otto'd go for corn cobs?"

"Is this you?" Magda asks. I'm still after that glass of water in the kitchen, but her soft clasp pulls me into another room that's used for ... well, apparently nothing. Doors and corridors branch off nowhere and everywhere in this house.

There's probably an entire floor somewhere people have forgotten about.

She points to a photo framed on the wall. Her other hand rubs inside my forearm.

"University rugby," I say. "I only played for about ten minutes. I was always too scared of the ball. Or too scared of the scrum. Or too scared –"

"Your *hair* is what is the scary thing," Magda interrupts, and stabs the glass with a fingernail.

In the faded photo I'm in the back row, wavy blond shoulder-length mid-'70s hair, toothy grin, eyes smiling at the camera. Otto stands beside me, carrot-top shaggy over a scraggly orange beard.

"We had a lot more hair in those days."

"It is the eldest photo at the wall," Magda notes.

She looks at me, then back at the photo. Then at me again, brilliant blue eyes piercing into my face. Then back at the photo.

I look at her, then at the photo again. Then at Magda again. "What're you looking at?"

"You were not such a good-looker then, I think."

I raise my eyebrows.

"But now, yes, I would fuck you now."

Indian

"Oh, hallo, sir? How are you, sir?"

I'd noticed the smell first, a spicy aroma wafting through the open front door, but as I pop my head around the corner and see him standing in the doorway, white plastic bags looped over his hand, I can't work out what the issue is.

"Hugh," says Magda, holding the doorhandle, "I do not know what this man says to me."

The man just outside the doorway looks at me, bewildered, too. "Sir, I am finding this lady not easy to understand."

The contrast – Magda's choppy rhythm; the delivery-man's sing-song – makes me smile. But I want to avoid an international incident.

"I am not understanding him."

"I am not understanding her."

"What language is he speaking, Hugh?"

"Does she speak English, sir?"

The wheels of recognition stir, but still … he could be any number of my ex-students. Some weeks I wonder if I haven't taught English as a Second Language to half the sub-continent.

"The bill is fifty-two dollars and forty-five cents, sir."

Magda holds the door open while I reach into my wallet and dole out fifty-two dollars and forty-five cents into the deliveryman's open palm.

"Are you here on holidays, sir?" he says, scrunching up the notes in one hand.

I take the plastic bags by the handles from his other hand. "With friends for the weekend."

"Thank you, sir. I wish you good eating, sir. Happy evening."

He disappears into the twilight as I close the door. Even with his back turned I still can't place him.

Kendalynn ladles the four dishes — brown and orange and red and green (the spinach choice, I assume), paid for by me as a thankyou — from their throwaway recyclable containers, into clay bowls.

The saffron rice and garlic naan and raita and other dishes Kendalynn and Otto habitually order from the Fleurieu Tandoor Bazaar on The Strand — "What do you feel like?" they asked us but somehow, whatever house, whatever location, they order the same menu as always — already wait on the twelve-seater glass-topped table, steam rising.

Otto pours the drinks — red wine for the three of us, white for Kendalynn — then watches, wide-eyed, as Magda commits the cardinal sin of immediately picking up her glass without allowing the wine time to breathe.

"But you did not know him," Magda says, holding the glass to her mouth, like she's teasing a response from Otto.

"But his voice was familiar though." I twist my glass, the bouquet – a fruity cabernet? though Otto loves merlot – flushing my nostrils.

"I could not understand his voice," she says into the glass, and sips. Then, "Twenty years I am speaking English and no words of his I can understand."

"He was polite to remember me," I counter, staring at her.

"No," Magda's chin sets. "He should learn a different accent so people may understand him. He is communicating when he cannot communicate."

"Hey, Magda," Otto butts in, "ever thought of getting a bit of one-on-one tutoring with your own English? 'Cause you're murdering it at the moment."

Kendalynn's ladle halts in mid-air. My glass stops mid-twist.

"No," says Magda, and she sips her wine. "But that is why my speaking is so charmful."

Scarf

"That's gorgeous, Magda."

"Yes, my father was an electrician."

Kendalynn – stacking dirty dishes into the dishwasher – looks up, unsure what to say or do next.

"She meant your scarf," I add.

Kendalynn closes the dishwasher and pushes a button. Water gushes into the machine. Otto uncorks another bottle with a pop.

"Yes, it's gorgeous," Kendalynn says.

Magda puts the zapper on the kitchen counter and looks at Kendalynn like she cannot believe what she is hearing. "It is from my daughter. It is her own design." She unwinds the scarf from her neck, one end draping on the floor. "Unfortunately, it is ridiculous."

"But it's your daughter's design," says Kendalynn.

"Yes," says Magda. "Always I am very proud of Birgit. But it is still ridiculous."

Kendalynn leans across the bench, fingers the scarf's brown softness and peers at the needlework. "What stitch is it, do you know?"

Magda snorts. "My daughter knows but she is thousands of kilometres in Munich making designs for things people will not wear. So she gives them to me."

Kendalynn rubs her hand on the wool. "It must be a cashmere or alpaca mix, it's so soft."

Magda unwraps the other end and hands it all to Kendalynn. "Please have it."

The scarf is long, and wide too, wider than a normal scarf, soft and woollen but a definite mud colour. Attached to the middle, knitted into it, is a hood, and close to the hood are purpose-built armholes, not ripped into it because it was a good idea at the time, but actually a proper part of the design.

"But it's your daughter's."

"Birgit made it for me and she was making me choose the colour but you must have it, you like it, you have it. I have more at Hugh's house."

Magda never says *home*. *Home* is her apartment in Berlin.

Kendalynn takes the scarf and putting the hood on her head first, wraps the ends around her neck.

"No," says Magda. And stepping to Kendalynn's side, takes her hand and pushes it through an armhole. Like an awkward windmill, Kendalynn bends her other arm, then pushes her other hand through the second armhole herself.

"But I couldn't," she says, "your daughter made it for you."

Magda throws one end of the scarf over Kendalynn's shoulder. "I tell you a secret," she says. "I choose this colour because it is so dull and ugly and brown I think no one will see me in it. So I am a bad mother, and you will do a favour for Birgit and me when you wear it."

Otto laughs, sniffing the cork. "I get your logic, Magda."

"And you know many people, Kendalynn. You are good advertising for my daughter."

"But Magda," Kendalynn says, twirling around so the scarf ends fly out like a helicopter. "It's too beautiful —"

"For God's sake, woman," Otto snaps, "she wants you to have it!"

"It is too ugly for me. It looks much better with you," Magda says. "I think Birgit designs stupid things. So take it and you help all three of us."

Otto and I, from the balcony, watch the two women walk down to the beach, Kendalynn's new gift wrapped round her neck, Magda carrying the zapper.

"Now let's get to the good stuff," Otto says, splashing wine into our glasses, "and not waste it on those who don't appreciate it."

I look out at the sea and sigh, wanting to be with Birgit's new retail ambassador and the bad mother, lighting their way into the night with the zapper.

Deluge

Out on the balcony, a bottle of Cab Sav later, Otto's eyes bead on my face.

"Sorry about barging in on you, mate," he says.

"Ah," I say. And stop. What else do you say?

No worries, it happens to the best of us.

No worries, hope you got something out of it.

No worries, we just kept on fucking.

Pounding sounds from the sea wash over us.

"No worries, mate," I say.

Otto reaches down beside his deck chair and, picking up another bottle, uncorks it with a pop. I look out at the black sky and smell the night breeze and listen to wine splashing into our glasses.

"Fucked if I know what women want," Otto says.

I breathe out. It's late and Otto has a bottle in his hand so it's bonding time.

Which only means one thing: regurgitating our shared history.

Which is the only thing we still have in common.

Which means more red wine. And I've had enough.

"I married Kendalynn twice — *twice!* — and I still can't figure out what makes her tick."

Kendalynn is Otto's second and fourth wife. In between he married her sister. His first wife is the mother of his daughters. She's not related to anyone.

"You know she used the settlement from the divorce – money *I* sweated over making – to get her first – her fucking *first* – facelift?"

Otto sips from his glass. I smile, and half tune out. I've heard this story before.

"You look at the photos from both our weddings," he says, lowering his glass so it's angled on his thigh, "and you were at both of 'em: it's like looking at a different woman! Almost didn't recognise her comin' down the aisle the second time."

I swirl the wine in my glass, so it threatens to spill over the rim.

"Now she's got some money from her aunt who died six months ago and she says she wants a nose job for her birthday. *Will it make you breathe better?* I said." He nods in self-agreement. "It's fuckin' fucked up, 'scuse the fuckin' French."

We pause as we wait for another brilliant idea to form in Otto's head.

"What do you give German women for their birthday?" He slurs on the word German, so it sounds more like *Geeerrrrrrrrrmannn*.

I snort. It's kind of funny and kind of not.

"Or what does a German woman give herself?" I say. "Last birthday Magda bought her own gift. So I got in early and have given her her *next* birthday present already."

Otto takes another gulp. "What'd she get herself?"

I look him in the eye. "Viagra."

Otto's mouth drops. "You're shitting me?"

We pause as we consider the next comment.

He shakes his head. "She's got a cock too?"

"No, no," I snort again – and I'm the one who's drunk less – or less drunk. "She got it for me to use."

He nods. "How was it?"

I shrug my shoulders and think of an answer. "It gave me a headache so I said *I've got a headache* and went to bed early."

Otto's throws his head back. His laughter booms across the starry sky.

Samoa

I did not care for Sybil's forgiveness.

"Hugh?"

Under the sheet, a foot rubs my calf.

I turn the page of the potboiler Kendalynn has lent me. It's one of the pleasures of beach holidays, lost in a book with silver lettering on the cover and lines of text too close together.

I had to do this now.

"Hugh, you should put down your book and put your penis inside my vagina."

Or I would not be able to forgive myself.

I read more words but they blur in my brain. "Haven't we done that already?"

Magda pulls herself up and rests her head on my shoulder, her chemise – the early birthday gift from me – smooth against my arm. "But it is now a new year and we must celebrate it."

"A new year where?"

"In Samoa."

"American Samoa or the former Western Samoa?"

Her knee hooks across my waist, and taking the book from my grasp, she snaps it shut.

Magda is on her back and I'm sliding into her. She's the wettest woman I've ever been with, even at forty-nine, a feat she is extraordinarily proud of. "I am lube-free," she often says, "I drink prune juice."

In and out, I work up a slow rhythm.

"I do not think Otto likes me."

The window is open. A night breeze, salty and fresh, blows over my arse and prickles the stubble across my back. Time for a new waxing, I think.

"I do not," Magda continues, ever-efficient at multi-tasking, "drink my wine properly. I do not," – she arches her back in a way that I never know if it's a performance or for real – "speak my English properly."

Maybe it's real *and* a performance.

She looks beautiful, blonde hair tousled about her face, tanned skin I know extends from her shoulders right down to her toes. She pulls her chemise up over her breasts and licking her fingers, caresses her ripe nipples, breasts flat and hanging down her sides. She knows I love this (*porn-star-sex*, she calls it) and then reaches up and pinches my own nipples. Hard. Between her pearly fingernails.

"And you are friends for many years with him."

I arc my back over her and groan.

"Maybe he thinks I do not fuck properly."

My balls churn. I want to cover her mouth with my hand but my hands are propping me up.

"He was I think making a score while he watched us fuck before." She smiles again. "He just —" but she gasps.

Again, is this real? I don't know. At the moment, her pussy feels too good for me to care.

Magda gasps again and her eyes widen. "You are a good fucker, Hugh."

OK, so she doesn't say that, but telepathically …

I slope down and kiss her. She opens her mouth, and her tongue tastes of mint. She opens her legs wider and I dive in deeper.

Which is not bad for a man of fifty-six. Give or take some Viagra.

Saturday

Morning

"This is my favourite time in Australia," she whispers, the breeze blowing her blonde hair so it frames her face when she looks at me. She only has to whisper and I can hear her, it's so quiet.

The sun is just above the horizon when our bare toes hit the soft sand. Low over the water and Middleton and beyond, it's not light enough for sunglasses so we push them onto the top of our heads. Everyone wears sunglasses in Australia, and even Magda wears them now, when she remembers.

("Leave the zapper behind," I'd said, and she did.)

She slips her hand into mine – I'm always happy to hold her hand but usually wait for her to take the initiative – and her shoulder bumps into mine as we step east: we're the same height and have similar strides so walking hand-in-hand is not the clown act it is with some couples.

The tide is high – I think, I'm not quite sure, tides and the moon were never strong points – but who cares? The sea is blue, we can hear waves crash on the rocks out at the head of the bay, and it promises to be a warm day. We wear light jumpers and already my back is slightly sticky.

We are the only people on the beach, I think, but then look up and ahead — way ahead, at the other end of the bay, in the distance — is a man on the edge of the water.

I squeeze Magda's hand.

"The colours are beautiful and everything is new," she adds.

"You bought the tourist cliché," I laugh.

She smiles.

We say nothing, strolling in sync, feet squeaking on the sand.

We walk past thatches of brown seaweed, thick and darkened and dried. They weren't there yesterday afternoon.

And draw closer to the man in the distance. He's fly-fishing. Which is odd on this beach, because it's not known for any kind of fishing but maybe he knows more than I do, especially as I don't like fishing.

He wears an old faded red jacket, and whips the rod and line behind him, then casts it out to sea.

"I think he's practicing casting," I say, surprised I know even that much.

We sit and watch him — he doesn't nod or say hello or smile — and five or ten or fifteen minutes later we stand up and head back.

*   *   *

Halfway back, and not a split second too soon, we step around a dead seagull. It's dead and it's a seagull, but beyond that, I don't want to know. How we didn't see it before, I don't know either.

Magda's hand slips out of mine and she kneels beside it.

"Don't touch it," I say.

"It is just a dead bird, Hugh." She looks up at me, squinting, her sunglasses still on her head. "We should perhaps bury her."

I push my hands into my pockets. My car keys would normally be in the right pocket and my mobile in the left, but now, they're empty. "The tide will come and take it out to sea."

"Yes," she says, and stands up. She holds out her hand and I clasp mine around it.

Walking up to the beach house, we see Valerie, Otto's daughter, slam the door of an old blue Subaru parked in the driveway. Its engine makes the ticking noise of a motor just turned off.

"Morning," she says. She wears an old yellow t-shirt and jeans, faded hennaed hair – her one concession to femininity – curly and piled on top of her head, stuck with a rubber band. "Thought I'd come down and give Dad the shits for a few days."

She reaches in through the Subaru's open window and grabs an old yellow backpack from the back seat.

"Oi, I'm here!" Valerie calls out (I presume to Otto and Kendalynn), shattering the morning calm.

And following behind her, her workboots scraping on the sandy tiles of the front porch, we walk inside.

Sugar-whacked

"I'm a tit woman," Valerie says, spooning *Frooty Whacks* into her mouth, red hair bobbing as she crunches and swallows. Soymilk — a carton sits on the twelve-seater glass-topped table by her bowl — dribbles down her chin.

Magda sits opposite, spooning *Seitenbacher Müsli* — sent every three months from Munich by her daughter — into her own mouth. I sip coffee from a white cup so over-generous it's bathroom basin-sized.

"But it is better to be a whole woman," Magda says, "and not just tits."

Otto bursts into laughter in the vast kitchen beside the dining area. He wheezes, bending over, turning away from the eggs and bacon he's cooking on the eight-burner stove, head bobbing down under my line of sight, hidden by the island cupboard. Laughing laughing laughing. Like every-thing in this house, the kitchen and eating area are spacious and overdone.

"Otto!" says Kendalynn, cutting open a grapefruit on a large cutting board. "You're getting grease on the tiles."

Otto stands up, wiping his eyes with the back of his hand, the designer titanium spatula in his other hand still dripping bacon fat onto the floor tiles (these tiles, the ones covering the kitchen and eating area) especially made (so Kendalynn told us last night) in a Lithuanian monastery.

"She means she likes women's breasts," I explain.

"I'm an arse man myself," Otto says. "I like something I can sink my teeth into. Hey, Kendalynn?"

Otto's laughter echoes around the vast room again. Kendalynn says nothing. And as she walks into the orgy-sized pantry, Otto pretends to smack her bottom with the spatula.

I sip my coffee as Valerie spoons more *Frooty Whacks* into her mouth. And hear the crunch as she forgets to close her mouth in time. For a woman who carries the weight of the world on her shoulders – gloomy eyes, determined chin, downturned snarl to her mouth – eating cereal made for kids, marketed at parents who care little about nutrition, is seriously surreal.

Valerie catches me watching the fluoro hoops swimming in soy. "I need the sugar hit, after the long drive here." And she nods in self-agreement.

"It's that job of yours," says Kendalynn, placing an antique silver saltcellar she must have taken from the pantry, and her grapefruit halves directly on the glass table. She pulls out a chair and sits down. "It's inhuman the hours you work."

"Not as bad as the lives of the women I help at the shelter."

Kendalynn opens the saltcellar and spoons salt – but the crystals look just a little too large for salt – over the grapefruit.

"Is that sugar?" asks Magda.

"No, no," Kendalynn says, holding a grapefruit half with her fingers. "The salt brings out the acid. It's very refreshing."

"Hmmph," says Otto at the stove.

Kendalynn pushes the spoon into the pale flesh. "And grapefruit's wonderful for the figure."

Magda opens her mouth to continue but a boom from the kitchen cuts her off.

"Stay under my roof, live by *my* fucking rules!" Otto yells, designer titanium spatula flicking bacon grease as he jabs it in his daughter's direction.

Valerie is on her feet with lightning speed, chair smacking against the Lithuanian tiles as she stabs the air with her finger. "My fucking life and my fucking beliefs and I do what I fucking want!"

"Not under this roof, missy!"

I don't know where to look, so I look at Kendalynn. Kendalynn looks over at Otto. I look at Magda. Magda looks at Otto and then at Valerie.

"Take that fucking badge off!" Otto yells.

I look at Valerie. She's wearing a small badge of a flag – mid-blue background with five stars, one along each edge and one smack in the middle, joined by a thick squashed +

— above her left breast. It's the Eureka flag, the Southern Cross beloved of the trade union movement.

"Fuck you, you money-grubbing bastard!" Valerie pushes her bowl of *Frooty Whacks* away. Her workboots pound on the tiles as she thunders out of the room.

The smell of burning bacon hits our nostrils. "Christ!" Otto yells, as he whisks the frying pan off the stove and throws it into the titanic ceramic sink filled with suds. It scorches on the water, hissing as it sinks, dirty clouds mushrooming to the ceiling.

Otto yells at the steaming breakfast — "I hate fucking burnt bacon!" — throws the spatula on top of the soggy, greasy mess, and shakes his head.

We watch him, spoons and cup mid-air, waiting for the next move.

"I blame myself." His voice is soft as he watches the steam ebb. "I shouldn't have divorced her mother. Things would have turned out a *whole* lot different, believe you me."

I look at Kendalynn, waiting for her reaction. She picks up Valerie's bowl and dumps her uneaten grapefruit in it, pushes her chair back, and takes the sloshing bowl over to the draining board. Then pulls the frying pan from the sink and reaches for the dishcloth.

I sip my coffee.

Magda licks a finger, dips it in the saltcellar, and licks the tip with her tongue.

"Sugar," she says, looking over at the kitchen. "Your supermarket sells you sugar, Kendalynn, but names it salt. They should pay you a refund."

Smoking Gun

Flicking through the book Kendalynn lent me last night –
rescued from its nesting place down the side of the armchair
– nothing grabs me. The trash lit. lure needs solitude and
smug enjoyment and neither are available here.

I look up as Magda, her t-shirt just covering her
bottom, glides her iron across her white shorts, the
rainwater she uses in the iron steaming the air with its fresh
eco-smell. The ironing board looks virgin-new, never-
used, a demo model without the demos or – more likely –
without the purpose. She'd grabbed it from the cupboard in
the laundry (the laundry next to the kitchen, not the
laundry next to the shed with all the beach equipment) and
set it up in the middle of the over-sized living room.

("You like a nice view when you're ironing?" Otto had
asked, looking through the picture window to the sea
outside as she set up the ironing board. Then at her arse as
she bent over and plugged the iron into the wall socket.

"It is the biggest room in your house," Magda replied.

"You like a lot of space when you're ironing, then?"

"Not always. Small rooms are good too.")

I watch Magda's biceps stretch and contract as the iron
steams across the thick fabric, under then over the cuffs,

along the fly, deep into the crotch. Eyes down, mouth slightly open, hair falling from behind her ears, she sits the iron down, rotates the shorts on the end of the ironing board, grabs the iron again and pressing it against the back pockets, squeezes a button and gives it a surge of steam.

"What are you reading, Hugh?" she asks.

"I wouldn't call it reading," I say, my leg over the arm of the armchair, foot swinging. "More like ... avoiding."

Otto walks in and sits at the end of the six-seater sofa again, soft white leather oomphing under his legs. He's cooked himself some more bacon and is eating it, wedged between two thick slices of toast.

Magda bends down and unplugs her iron from the socket.

"No, no," says Otto, watching her arse again, bacon grease on his lips. "Don't let me stop you."

"I am not stopping, I am finished." Magda places the iron on the ironing board to cool, folds her shorts in half along the main seam and lays them on the ironing board too.

She picks up the plastic jug she uses for the water, from the coffee table between Otto and me, and reaches for the iron to take it back to the bedroom and –

"That's a pretty impressive iron you got there, Magda."

Magda stops and looks at Otto as he bites into his bacon sandwich again. Towering over him, iron in hand, cord unfurling, she could easily drop the hot iron in his lap or sear it into his face.

"It is expensive but good quality is always expensive."
She looks at it, as if for the first time, and her eyes open
wide, almost in wonder. "And it is very environmental too,
made of recycled plastic and not heavy." Her eyes darken.
"But you can only use rain water with it, so it is lucky you
have three rain water tanks in your garden also. It is nice
for your guests."

Otto swallows. "And it's cheap to run?" he asks.

"Yes, that is a good thing too. It is very efficient with
energy."

Otto sits back in the armchair. "'Course it would be
even more energy efficient if you didn't iron your shorts
every day."

Magda cocks her head. I hold my breath. For all his
own bravado, Otto is still our host.

"Yes," says Magda. "But then you would not have the
pleasure of seeing me as I am bending over and unplugging
my iron."

She smiles, blows on the iron like a gun, and walks
through the door into the hallway.

Build

"I needed to get my magazines, sorry," Kendalynn says, flopping into the seat next to me. "Aahhh," she sighs. "Now, where was I?"

I stretch my feet on the sand in front of my chair, and bite again into my mid-morning apple. A mother, holding her young children by their hands as if they're on a leash, walks past, chatting on their way to the water's edge.

"There is no use apologising, Kendalynn," Magda says, sitting on my other side. "It is your house and your beach."

Kendalynn squirms her bottom into the seat so it settles into the sand. "Magda, you say the nicest things."

Magda tucks her head back into her book – Isaac Asimov, but in German – while Kendalynn pushes her diamante sunglasses further along her nose and opens a magazine on her lap. I look at the sea. The view is marred by Valerie and Otto – no word passing between them – on their knees, sweaty backs to each other, arse cracks damp in their shorts, building sandcastles. If I wasn't such a voyeur I'd move away in horror but the air reeks of salt and testosterone and I can't decide what I'd rather do instead.

"Oh, I left my hat behind," Kendalynn sighs. "There's always something." But still she sits, making no move to move. And pulls out a purple pen, clipped inside her magazine.

I bite into my apple again. Valerie wears a t-shirt emblazoned with the Eureka flag, breasts billowing bra-less underneath – "You don't own the beach, too, Dad," she'd said in her one concession to open communication. "No sir-fucking-ree! Up the workers!" – while Otto wears a crisp white polo shirt, the collar turned up behind his sun-browned neck.

Kneeling, Valerie drips wet sand above a mound made with an upturned bucket, creating a pretty tower. Her sandcastle is more ornate, turreted, with a dried seaweed drawbridge, but her father's is bigger, messy lines blurring the edge of the castle with the edge of the rest of the world.

"I guess it's telling me something," Kendalynn adds. She draws a circle in purple pen around a picture of a purple handbag in her magazine. Which, I now realise, is not a magazine as she said, but a shopping catalogue.

"I can never decide which style of hat suits me," Kendalynn sighs. "Picture hats make my head look small but they keep the sun off. And hats that are floppy always look" – she rings a purple lamp with her purple pen – "too floppy."

Otto turns and looks at his daughter's sandcastle, pointing at another turret. "Missed a bit there," he says.

Valerie points at her father's head. "Missing a bit there, too."

"What do you think about hats, Magda?" Kendalynn peers at Magda over her diamante sunglasses and squints into the sun.

Magda looks up from her book. "You want me advising you?"

I breathe in, sinking in my chair, dreading Magda's answer.

"I know nothing by Australian fashions." But her tone is soft and she sounds … well, interested. "I love all the bright colours in Australia but I cannot wear them. I am German. I can wear black and grey and brown and in summer white but nothing else. With any other colour I am an impoaster."

"*Impostor*," I say, snapping the last bite.

"I would be an *impostor* if I said *impostor* when I mean *impoastor*," Magda adds, "Hugh."

"There's no such word as *impoaster*," I say through masticating apple.

"Then Kendalynn will hear my mistake and know my real meanings."

"Oh good," Kendalynn cuts in, reading from her 'magazine'. "Apparently if you stand next to a cow it's very slimming."

My mouth open to ask which breed of cow, I stop, and swallowing the last of my apple, toss the core onto the sand in front of me and push it under with my big toe.

Kids

"What do you want for lunch?"

"I do not know, Hugh. What do you want for lunch?"

"I don't know." I turn to Valerie, now wearing a white t-shirt with *Fuck the Ritch* across her breasts. Except her breasts – they're still bra-less – push the *Ritch* underneath so if you want to read the whole message, you have to crane your head and … well, it's complicated.

I'm hoping for some inspiration from Valerie but her hands are dipping into a packet of Beefy Tomato chips, so it's not promising.

"What do you feel like Valerie?"

"Ah, I'm not fussy," she says, wiping her hand across her stomach, leaving a dusty red smear on her t-shirt, the chip packet crinkling. I notice she notices I've noticed this – I look at her, she looks back, I return the look – but still I say nothing. "Food would be good," she adds.

We've been left to our own devices.

("Can you kids amuse yourselves for a few hours?" Kendalynn had asked. "We need to go and see someone about something.")

Someone about something? And *kids*? Where did *kids* come from?

"She just gets off on the mothering thing," Valerie explained, standing beside the island cupboard in the Great Hall of the People aka the kitchen, wrapping her hands in the waistband of her t-shirt, stretching it. "Her ovaries are fried but her brain doesn't always register that." And she nodded in self-agreement.

"I have two adult children and I never have said *kids* to them," said Magda, standing on the other side of the cupboard.

"Do they have the word *kids* in German?" Valerie asked.

"No.")

Now we are in the mammoth pantry. There are lots of packets, neatly organised but uninspiring – rice dinners and sauce sachets and heat-and-eat noodles on the left; flavoured custards and jellies and pavlova cases in front; dried skim milk and cereals and dry biscuits on the right. Above these are tins, organised on the same lines: peaches and apricots and fruit salad mix in front; on the left, peas and asparagus and three bean mix and four bean mix and five bean mix and something I thought had been banned by the Food Police, camp pie. And on the right, bottles and jars of pickles and onions and olives and tomato sauce and barbecue sauce and Worcestershire sauce. There's so much food here, it's enough to intimidate you into never staying in and going out for every meal: the choice is easier outside.

"Was Kendalynn preparing something?" Magda asks, eyes running along the packets of dessert puddings. "Maybe there is some fruit."

"Yeah, grapefruit with salt," laughs Valerie, her mouth full of chips again, some spraying and sticking to her chin. Really, the chips just won't quit.

We watch her as her laughter peters out. And I notice for the first time, as she picks chip shards from her back teeth with an index finger, she has the same front teeth as her father, small and incisive.

"I get enough fruit from my Frooty Whacks, anyway," Valerie adds. Her eyes stray to a collection of Cup-a-Soups on the right. "Don't get me wrong, I like Kendalynn. But the best thing that can be said about her is, you get what you pay for."

Before I know it, it's out in the open: "You sound just like Otto."

Valerie's mouth drops. She looks at me, jaw flapping but nothing coming out, with a mixture of shock and ... more shock. Her eyeteeth, I see, are small, yes, but like daggers. She closes her mouth and swallows.

Magda puts her hand on my elbow. "You must apologise, Hugh."

Valerie opens her mouth to speak but her mobile rings in her pocket, so she pulls it out and answers the call. Which, luckily, is easier than the truth I've just blurted out.

"Yeah? Hi. Yes, well, that's a really good point socially."

Valerie is lost in her 'phone call, eyes on the ceiling but not really looking.

I breathe in — the overwhelming smell is of cardboard — and glance at my watch.

"What?!" She swings away from us, towards the pasta snacks, head down, perhaps looking at her feet. It gives her no privacy but maybe she's not really interested in that anyway.

I take the six steps necessary to retreat to the pantry doorway, and look at Magda. Magda's eyes are on the back of Valerie's head.

"What the fuck?!" Valerie says. "No no no no fucking fucking NO!"

"Magda," I whisper. She turns and looks at me, wondering why — of all the times and places — I would whisper to her now.

"Trudy, you had better say NO! She's my ex- and I don't care how many days it's been."

I cock my head in the direction of everywhere else. Magda nods and walks out behind me.

Upstairs, we grab our backpacks from the ottoman by the window overlooking the street. I stand at the top of the staircase, placing my cap on my head, wondering how much noise we should make: a lot, so Valerie knows we're leaving? Or none, in deference to her drama? Does good guest etiquette extend to the host's daughter's explosive lovelife?

We step outside and hear Valerie's voice boom from the pantry. "Get your own pussy!"

We start walking up the hill and into the town. A breeze blows behind us and as I look over my shoulder through my sunglasses, white froth bursts on the sand.

"We are eating lamb in the evening," Magda says. "And lamb is very fatty so we should eat nothing now. Yes?"

The problem is I don't want to eat nothing now either. "The stomach wants what it wants," I say.

"Yes, that is true also," Magda adds. She strides next to me and, just as I smell the apple of her shampoo, slips her hand inside mine.

Broken

"I'm not convinced she's a lesbian," says Valerie, now wearing black Spandex pedal-pushers, a pink and orange striped t-shirt and a glimpse of eyeliner at the end of her eyelids.

I reach over and pick up a vase from a glass shelf. The shelf wobbles as I lift it off, and I hold my breath for a split second, hoping the shelf won't fall.

"She's a big fat fake," Valerie adds.

I turn the vase in my hands. It's purpley-blue, with a sheen, and in its curved reflection, I see the cloth cap perched on my head.

"She said she wouldn't go out with my ex- but I don't trust her. She's got a lot of catch-up fucking to do."

The doorbell tinkles as another customer enters the shop. Each time the door opens – and the warm weekend weather has made Sappho Antiques quite popular today – a fresh breeze wafts through, disturbing the stale, dusty, fusty warm smell antique shop-owners love.

"Weight has never been one problem for Trudy, has it?" Magda asks.

"She just thinks it's the latest fashion and she wants to be *in*." Hands on her hips, Valerie stares Magda down, daring her to disagree.

The vase makes me think of Kendalynn and her circling purple items in shopping catalogues with a purple pen. But there's a chip, a fleck of white around the rim of the vase and I place it back on the shelf. I could offer half price, but then I'd still have to pay for it.

"She's just a copycat." Valerie is still on topic. "She should just realise muff is not her taste and moo-*oove* on."

I push my hands in my pockets. The smell of the shop is closing in on me and I frown. "Is there a test you can take?"

Of course I'm joking, trying to lighten my own mood as much as anything. But truth be told, Otto's other daughter makes a much more convincing lesbian than Valerie. Cropped hair, a throaty laugh and florid fashion sense, after three husbands and four children over ten years and a *Finding your inner goddess* retreat, Trudy finally told the world what we had all suspected since she was sixteen and spending all her spare waking hours attending a girls' youth group at the local church.

Valerie, in comparison, just looks frumpy and grim.

But Valerie takes this rivalry with her younger sister very seriously.

"I was the one who came out first," Valerie says. "Whoever said imitation is the sincerest form of flattery is full of the sincerest shit."

Magda sighs. "Ah, it was long years ago but I was a lesbian once."

Valerie and I snap our heads to look at her.

"Then that summer job ended and I went back to Berlin."

Valerie's eyes have widened at this revelation. Is it my imagination, or are her breasts, suddenly, visibly perkier under their pink and orange stripes?

"But there was no sex except for dildos!" Magda continues. "There was too many rubber and plastic and I did not want to commit myself to something I could not later get rid of."

I can't gauge from her expression – blank but serious – how true this is.

A smile tickles the corners of Valerie's mouth. She looks the happiest – or the least genuinely unhappy – she has looked all day. "Would you go back to it?" she asks.

"Ugh, no." Magda brushes her blonde hair off her face, sniffs, dips her hands into a box of old buttons. "It was the seventies. If I had known about that lesbian test, I would have saved myself from a lot of body stench and that horrible nipples rash."

Schmutzig

"Mein Deutsch ist Scheiße."

"Yeah?" asks Valerie. "Why do you say that?"

I look at her, unsure if she understands what I've just said.

"I've got no idea what you've just said," she adds, "but it sounds like you're talking shit."

I look up The Strand, the town's quiet main street, up the slow hill towards the cliff top that leads up and over to the sea. Magda sits on the kerb outside the stained glass studio-shop, leaning back against a verandah post, her feet in the gutter. She's talking on her mobile – as she does three times a week – to her son Jörg in Berlin.

Despite the nine and a half hour time difference so it's 4.45am Saturday there and 2.15pm Saturday here.

Straining to listen to her conversation, I strain just as much to appear casual – wiping my forehead with the back of my hand and touching the sweaty tip of my nose with a crooked knuckle – while listening.

"*Ich glaube dich, Jörgchen, aber ...*" and then the rest is lost in a guttural string.

"She thinks something," I tell Valerie, and lean slightly on my left foot towards Magda. Pretending to stretch my Achilles tendon.

Valerie adjusts her bra strap under her orange and pink striped t-shirt and I notice not only is she wearing a bra – I can now see the bra strap indentation on each shoulder – but she also has a fringe – damp, faded henna – stuck to her forehead. She's a woman in her early thirties with a fringe.

"No," I add, "she *believes* something."

"*Ja, ja, ja, ich verstehe, aber wo ist dein Geld?*" Magda says. Or something approaching that.

"Is she angry?" Valerie asks. She has a smug look on her face, like she's pleased someone else has a not-so-good personal life.

I shrug my shoulders. "*Jein.* Jörg's always going on spending sprees and buying old East German cars to do up."

Valerie nods, probably because I sound convincing.

Of course not only is my German shit but Valerie's right, I'm talking shit in English too. After each 'phone call Magda turns pale and her eyes are dark and troubled. And she says nothing.

"*Unglaublich!*" Magda says.

Valerie nods in Magda's direction. "She sounds like she means it."

I smile and stare at the bitumen footpath between my sports shoes. I smile because I really hate the conversations

Magda has with Jörg. They're a part of her life I'm not part of. And I smile because hating it makes me uncomfortable.

And Valerie is still smiling too, probably because she sees my discomfort. And there's that lesbian nipples rash revelation, too.

Coffee wafts from the café two doors up the hill. "Coffee'd be nice," I say, and Valerie nods and looks at her watch.

"Kaffee, Magda?" I ask, breaking in to her conversation.

"Ja, ja," Magda says, covering her ear with her hand.

I push my thumbs into my pockets. My cap is sticky on my head. "She won't be long."

A breeze rustles a rainbow windsock hanging from the verandah post.

"Okay, okay," Magda says. And like a chime, louder than the rest of her conversation – and I can hear Jörg say it with her in unison, in English – *"The empire thanks you."*

I never know what that means but Magda taps her mobile shut, stands up and looks directly at me. "Kaffee?" she says.

"Natürlich."

She brushes her bottom. And says something that she would never say in Germany, it's too vulgar, but it's funny how people change in a new environment: "Mein Arsch ist schmutzig, Hugh."

So I step behind her and brush her bottom too.

Coffee

The menu chalkboard has so many rubbings-out I can't see what's on, what's off, and what's smeared bird shit. And the inviting coffee smell has been replaced by stale café and burnt cheese.

We sit beside an open window. It's the only unoccupied table beside an open window. At other tables sit a bored-looking older couple, little in common except their mutual boredom, both nursing cappuccinos and solemn, hangdog expressions; and a boring-looking blond surfer – whose slouching spread, idiot grin and sun-bleached straw-for-hair scream 'dude' – looking at the pictures in a surfing magazine. A fruit juice bottle lolls on its side by his hand. The sun shines in directly on our table so it's hot but I'm hopeful a breeze will blow through the window and cool our faces and ease some of the stale café and burnt cheese stink.

The waitress, young and thin and tanned and warm weekend busy with a blue cloth wrapped around her waist – really, it looks just like an extra long tea towel – takes out her pen and pad.

"Milchkaffee, bitte," Magda says before the waitress opens her mouth, her mind still on the 'phone to Berlin. She places her mobile on the table beside my upturned cap, and stares at it.

The waitress looks at me for confirmation.

"A flat white, she means," I say, spotting a *trainee* badge above her shirt pocket, "and a long black for me, please."

"Yes, one times a flat white," says Magda, "but not such a flat white, a flat*tish* white." She looks at the waitress, daring her to assert her right to exist.

The waitress, hesitating, dips her head and writes on her pad, the letters slow and deliberate. She opens her mouth to speak again but Valerie is ready with a smile.

"Could you do me a combo?" she asks, her eyes flickering at the waitress's breasts.

How old is the waitress? Twenty? Twenty-two? But her breasts are ripe and pillowing under her tight white blouse. Sensing a takeover, she clutches her pad closer to her cleavage.

"I'd really like a raspberry mocha thickshake," Valerie says, and breathes out. "Could you do me one of those?"

The waitress looks at Valerie like she too is speaking German. And her pad drops a little. "I don't know what that is. I don't think we do those."

Valerie smiles wider, her top lip covering her pointy teeth. (My God, Otto does exactly the same thing!) And breathes in. "Just a water then, thanks."

The waitress writes again, pressing the pen deep into the paper, every rounded letter a work of art. I half-expect to see her pen nib scraping through the other side of the cardboard. It's not the only impression she's making. And then: "I'll be with you shortly."

"She's sweet," Valerie sighs, drumming her fingers on the table, watching her back disappear. "I think I know her."

"Her breasts you know very well," Magda says. "We know now you are certainly a tits woman."

Valerie stops her finger-drumming. Her nails are short and practical, the barest crescent peaking over each tip.

Magda sighs. Her eyes darting inside her head, are dark and hooded. She picks up her mobile then puts it back down again beside my cap, unsure and restless, hands fidgeting.

Then throws her hands in the air. "Tits, tits, tits!" she continues. "Tits everywhere for you, Valerie. You get an operation you have tits on your back also." She stabs the table with her finger. "More fun for you too."

Valerie moves closer so her face edges over the table, level with Magda's. "If you're gonna insult me Magda, use proper fucking English!"

Magda sits back in her chair, shakes her head. "Everyone is so *sensibel* in this country."

The waitress behind the counter stares, bog-eyed.

"Hugh's an *English language teacher* and you can't even speak it properly. You're a bad advertisement for him!"

Valerie says <u>ad</u>-*va*-*tize*-*ment*, the way I loathe. I say *ad*-<u>ver</u>-*tez*-*ment*, which is what I teach. Inwardly, I shudder. Maybe outwardly, I shudder too.

I look around at the other customers still in the café. The dude is smirking into his magazine but the dull couple have their hangdog heads skimming just above their flagging cappuccinos.

The waitress stands behind the coffee machine. Her eyes are moist and her mouth quivers. Perhaps it's her first day on the job. She reaches under the counter. To press a panic button?

"Your bad English is *bullshit*," Valerie says. "You *choose* to speak badly because you think it makes you *special*. And everyone knows you're a big fake too. *Everyone*." And her eyes flick at me.

"Is this true, Hugh?" Magda glares, goading me to reply.

I pause.

"Is this *true?*" Magda repeats. "Say the truth."

My mouth half-open, "Er," I say.

Magda slaps her hand on the table. "So I am a bad speaker of English. Shoot me for dead and leave me on the beach then. Good-bye." She grabs her 'phone, throws her chair back and charges at the café door.

The waitress cowers behind the counter as Magda slams the door behind her. The young woman waits for what must be forever – she stares at us, mouth open. Is she scared

Magda will return? — then says, in a squeaky voice, "Does she want her flattish white to take away?"

Am Gendarmenmarkt

"I have to go back to Australia," I said.

The upturned collar of my polo shirt graced my neck as I looked through the window of the Schokoladen-Café onto sunny Gendarmenmarkt. The central Berlin square is my favourite place in the city. With two cathedrals in the middle – the Deustsche Dom and the Französische Dom – and the Konzerthaus in between, the Friedrichstadt neighbourhood was established in the late 1600s and named for Friedrich I. Many immigrant Huguenots had lived in the area too, hence the names Gendarmenmarkt and nearby Französische Straße. Much has been restored since the Wall came down.

Once a History teacher …

I dipped my spoon in the remains of the molten chocolate, thick and smooth and gluttonous and utterly delicious. And now, scraping the bottom of the small cup – a demitasse? What's the German for *demitasse?* – I shuddered at the thought of the rich taste on my tongue again. There's a reason they only serve it in small cups.

Is the chocolate a drink, a soup, a dessert? Whatever, visiting Fassbender und Rausch again was an anniversary treat, marking the two years since we'd met, since our first impromptu date to the very same chocolatier.

No gifts. Just chocolate.

I looked across at Magda, pale blue long-sleeved t-shirt sculpted across her shoulders and scooped over her cleavage. The morning sun shone down Mohrenstraße behind her and I wondered how I might have broached the subject better.

I <u>need</u> to go back to Australia?

I <u>should</u> go back to Australia?

I <u>must</u> go back to Australia?

Guess what, there's something I have to tell you and it ends with Australia?

Once an English as a Second Language teacher …

"I don't know how long for," I said. "My mother's sick and nearly ninety and when she goes I'll have to sort a lot of things out. And there's only me to do it." I shrugged my shoulders but could not look at her as I spoke. She knew I was an only child but still … so I looked down at my cup. Just the bare scrapings of a taste. And I didn't want to prise the glaze off and make an unpleasant noise – this was Germany after all, where no one likes a disturbance – so I laid the spoon on the plate. "She's lived in the house longer than I've been alive."

I looked up. Magda said nothing, but as she dipped her gaze to look deeper into her own cup, I saw an extra brightness in her eyes.

"Magda –"

"Yes, I am hearing you, Hugh." Magda looked out at Mohrenstraße, her eyes so blue in the light and sighed. "Ich mache das immer gerne ausländische Männer. Leider."

I nodded. After her Irish ex-husband she spent seven years on-and-off with a Czech diplomat. And relationships with foreigners? Yes, I know that deal.

"Birgit makes clothes that no one is buying but she is also very successful. Jörg is not successful but he is happy so he has maybe his own success."

Balancing in my seat, still not wanting to make any noise, I placed my hands under the table and stuck them, palms inwards, between my knees.

Magda looked me in the eye for the first time since I'd blurted out my plan. She blinked. Her eyes, so clear, showed no trace of tears now. But her chin quivered, just a little. "You want me to be coming with you?"

"Oh, yes!" I said, breathing out, my body relaxing into the back of the chair as relief flooded through me. I hadn't realised I was holding everything in. "Of course, I want you to come with me. I was telling the school that when I said I'd have to leave."

I'd also said, *Four years with the same language school is a good run. And I've outlasted many many many of my colleagues.*

Pulling my hands from between my knees, I reached across the table.

"I cannot be making my children's success." Magda dipped her spoon again into her cup, and giving me the handle, pointed the tip of the chocolate towards herself. "Eat me," she said.

She knew she was making a mistake, and she knew I knew she was making a mistake, but I smiled and she smiled and leaning forward, she opened her mouth.

In Memoriam

Does she want me to find her, I wonder?

My sunglasses slip to the end of my nose, the brim of my cap a darting silhouette on the bitumen, Achilles tendons stretching as I trudge up the slow incline to Commodore Reserve. I think that's where she headed, towards the end of The Strand and the park overlooking the cliff and the sea.

Or does she *not* want me to find her?

A breeze blows down the street. My t-shirt is sticky under my armpits.

Do *I* want to find her?

As I step towards Commodore Reserve — flat and barren, the lone white building a desolate toilet block, bushes along the perimeter shaped by wind off the sea — I see the park is empty.

I pull out my mobile and look at it shielded by my shadow — no, I was right: she hasn't messaged me.

Walking down the street again — Valerie, in her pink and orange striped t-shirt and sipping from a big plastic cup, looks in a shop window off in the distance — I turn right, heading for the bay. I don't know where I'm going except it's towards Otto's palazzo. This street, Murray

Place, is steep, and as I veer left I have to stop myself from falling into a downwards run, and there's no real footpath either. I step more than walk down the lumpy bitumen, and then see over to the right, in the long shade cast by Norfolk Island pines closer to the beach, between two bushes turned into a choppy, ill-advised hedge, a pathway, an entrance, a shortcut to the foreshore.

Crossing the road, I step through the entrance, down damp stairs and onto a lawned terrace. More steps and I'm down on the next terrace, green and spongy, and further down the garden, on the bottom terrace, I see the top of Magda's blonde head.

She's kneeling on the ground beside a memorial plaque when I reach her. There's a line of plaques, bronze and impersonal and smacking of renovation, set in the earth in front of a row of Norfolk Island pines, discarded fronds dried and littering the ground.

"Look," says Magda. "He has a better mother than me."

The memorial plaque celebrates the life and service of a man *Killed in Middle East* in 1942, as it says. (But the Middle East is so big! Which part?) And the surname is unmistakable: O'Grady. The name Magda once shared with her now ex-husband. The one she met in Germany and then left to live with in Ireland. Who had two children with her and who gave them this very same surname too.

I look left and right along the row and see the ground around each plaque is as well-tended as the one for this *Sgt. Pilot, 14 Sqdn, R.A.A.F.*.

"A good mother would come here every week and give new flowers," Magda says.

Standing at her shoulder, I do what I always do at moments like this — I shove my hands into my pockets. Magda pulls out weeds, lifts roots and all from the dirt, then throws the handful behind the pine trunk.

"A good mother would not let her son go to the war," she says. She brushes the dirt from her hands and stands up. The dirt smells damp and earthy, despite the afternoon heat — the majestic Norfolk Island pines provide canopies of vast shade.

Now she's standing beside me, I look into Magda's face and wonder if I dare pull away the stray blonde hair stuck to the corner of her mouth. But her hand pulls it away instead.

"A good mother would be there to support her son and to guide him through his life."

She turns her gaze to the plaque again and I know that I can't ever, not really, compete with her children, at least not her son Jörg.

She turns, and starts to walk down the row of pines. With loping steps, I catch up.

She sighs, and walking beside me, but just far enough apart to create an uncomfortable space, she says, "But I am not such a mother."

Dream

"I can't believe it, he's not taking the money!" Valerie says. And cupping her hands, she yells "The money! The money! Take the money!" at the television in the corner of the room.

"Take the money," Kendalynn joins in, then giggles.

"I can't believe he didn't take the money," says Valerie, shrugging her shoulders. "His luck's already started to run out." She picks up the remote and the television flickers off.

Kendalynn sighs, standing behind the island cupboard with a vegetable peeler in her hand. "It does seem a little silly yelling at a game show when we know it's a repeat."

I nod, but not because I care. Nursing another huge cup of coffee, I'm looking at the vase I saw my cloth cap reflected in at Sappho Antiques. It stands in the middle of the table – which doesn't do it justice, as the twelve-seater glass top makes it look smaller. But it's unmistakable: there's that chip on the rim.

"As I was saying before our excitement," Kendalynn says, "I can never really warm to celery."

It's hopeless: Kendalynn's voice is sing-song insistent, burning into your brain and dragging you into her stratosphere.

"Have you tried?" I ask. Being a good guest, I am not helping with the preparation of dinner. Magda is being an even better guest by lying down upstairs.

"Oh, *every* winter I *try*, but it's never any good," she replies, peeling a carrot, thin strips pooling on the counter-top. "Celery soup, celery in stir fries, celery in stuffing, celery in ..."

Sitting at the dining table, the smell of coffee wafts up from my cup and I imagine sticks of celery coming to Kendalynn in her dreams at night, leafy fronds caressing her cheek, begging her to love them.

"Or maybe it's *celeriac* I don't like," she says. "Oh dear, I can't remember." Her hand flies to her forehead, thinking. "Which one is it I don't like, Valerie? Celery or celeriac?"

Valerie is lost somewhere in the pantry. "Why would I know?" Her voice sounds like she might be found in the Cup-a-Soups.

"I'll have to keep my product knowledge up-to-date when the new venture starts up," Kendalynn adds. And looking at me, she shrugs her shoulders and gives a goofy grin. "It's really the beginning of something big." She looks across at the vase on the table and smiles. "And who better to be the chief business advisor than the award-winning businessman Mr Peter Otto."

Otto – and I often forget *Otto* is actually his surname – is pouring himself a glass of shiraz at the other end of the long kitchen counter. He raises his eyebrows. "It's her money."

"I saw it there on that wobbly glass shelf," Kendalynn says, picking up another carrot, "and it's purple and it was a sign, I think, an omen."

I see the white chip in the rim and wonder: good omen or bad?

Valerie, returned from the wilderness of the pantry, tosses a sachet on the counter. It skids to a stop beside Kendalynn.

"Diet chunky rosemary and garlic gravy," Kendalynn says, reading the packet, like she's seeing it for the first time, though she would have been the one who bought it. "That sounds nice."

"So is the rosemary powder chunky and the garlic powder low fat?" Valerie asks. "Or both powders low fat or is one *more* low fat than the other?" She's wearing another t-shirt, with *Daddy's Little Devil* painted across it. Her shoulders are still indented so she's still wearing her bra.

"It's pretty chunky if you make it with ice," I say.

"It's been my dream for a long time," Kendalynn continues, still in her own world. "Here in Port Elliot, an exclusive boutique-cum-general store, just selling purple things. A sort of weekend hobby store, to give something back to the community."

It's out of my mouth before I realise it. "Isn't that called *making a profit out of the community?*"

"So where's it going to be, this shop of purple things?" Valerie hasn't been listening to Kendalynn either. No one's listening to anyone here, really. Which is good, as I'm finding it harder to stop my thoughts from exploding out of my head.

"I'm going to buy the house where Sappho Antiques is. I'm going to rename it *Rainbow*."

The back door bangs against the outside wall as Otto walks out to start the barbecue, and I stare again at the vase on the table. It looked purpley-blue in the shop but it's looking more bluey-purple here in the interior light. Actually *completely blue* would be more accurate.

"This isn't lamb." Valerie – who's just had her head in the fridge – has a half-unwrapped slab of meat in her hand.

"It says lamb on the label," Kendalynn adds. And carrot still in hand, closes the fridge door Valerie left open.

"I know, but look at it," and Valerie thrusts the meat at Kendalynn's face. "It's beef."

"But it says lamb on the label."

"Sniff it!"

Kendalynn puts the carrot down on the countertop and flips over the plastic wrapping. While Valerie still holds it in her hand, Kendalynn draws her finger along the label. "See: *laaaamb*."

"My God, Kendalynn." Valerie, brown eyes bulging, looks like she wants to pulverise the meat into the counter-top in frustration. "Look at it, woman! It's beef!"

I stand up, coffee cup in hand, and cross to the warzone. And it's red, the roast is definitely beef, it's not the pinky-brown of lamb. "It's beef," I say.

"How did that happen?" Kendalynn asks.

"I guess it just morphed while it was in the fridge," Valerie says. "A bit like a butterfly turning into a caterpillar."

I look at them over the rim as I drain my cup.

"But I don't want a beef roast. We were saying on the way down here yesterday we were looking forward to a lamb roast. We promised Hugh and Magda a lamb roast."

"You should be making the roast beef in a pie."

It's Magda, sidling up to me, rubbing her eyes with the tips of her middle fingers, from the bridge of her nose – as she does – out towards her temples. But her expression is still sour, dull eyes and downturned mouth. This could be the expression she's still wearing when we leave tomorrow.

"I will make it in a pie. I make pies always at Hugh's house. I love pies."

It's odd but true: pies are not part of German cuisine. Pies are British and French and yes, Australian, sweet and savoury, but they don't make them in Germany. *If a German woman offers you a German pie, then she is an impoaster or the pie is an impoaster or both are impoasters*, Magda says. And over the last two years, outside Germany, she has grown to adore them.

And she loves to make the pie from scratch, with the butter and flour and egg and rolling the pastry on the kitchen bench – or better still, on the marble pastry board – with a rolling pin and arm muscles undulating and sweat beading on her forehead and slow-cooking the meat and gravy and brushing the top with egg or melted butter and serving it hot, in a pie dish placed in the middle of the table, steam rising through the top as you sink a serving spoon into it, pulling the pastry lid back and seeing the gravy bubbling underneath and the smiles appear and the smell of meat and butter and flour filling the room.

"Are you sure?" Kendalynn says.

Please, *please*, I think as I put my empty cup down, give her – Magda – something to make her feel useful and shift her mood.

"I don't think we have any pastry sheets in the freezer, Magda," Kendalynn says.

"What's in the freezer?" Otto asks through the open window, still outside, chest high above the windowsill. He's shaded by the verandah as he glugs at his glass of shiraz.

"It's not a lamb roast we bought, it's beef," Kendalynn says.

"Well, we won't be cooking anything in the barbecue anyway," Otto says, "'cause the gas connector's buggered."

Valerie steps towards the window. "What's wrong with it?"

"Got a bloody split in it." Considering the nuisance factor, I'm surprised Otto isn't more annoyed than he is. Perhaps the shiraz is working well already.

Kendalynn shakes her head. "So much for …" but she stops, unsure what she is so-muching for.

Valerie places the beef roast on the countertop and walks out through the back door. I watch her, through the window, walk behind her father, and disappear.

"What's she doing?" Otto asks as he watches her. He can see her where we can't – I'm still standing between the twelve-seater dining table and the island cupboard, next to Magda.

No one answers him.

So Otto swigs from his glass again.

Sounds of a car door creaking open come from outside.

"What the fuck's she doing?" Otto says.

Kendalynn looks around the kitchen. Then not finding anything better to do, wraps the erroneously-labelled plastic around the beef roast.

Sounds of a car door slamming shut come from outside.

And Valerie walks back into the window frame waving what looks like, from where I still stand inside, a small gas connector in her hand. She says nothing, as she and Otto disappear, crouching beneath the window ledge.

Kendalynn watches at the window. I look at Magda still standing beside me. Whose expression is granite.

Moments later we hear, "You bloody ripper!" from Otto, and his face reappears at the window. "The things she keeps in that shitbox Subaru. Still, she grew up in the hardware business." And he laughs. "Where's the beef roast? How long d'you reckon she'll take? And can you get Valerie a beer, love? She deserves one."

I look at Magda, and wonder how many rocks I could crack on her face. And seconds later I hear her footsteps on the stairs, pie-making a dead issue.

Kendalynn holds the beef roast aloft like a spoil of war and takes it out to the barbecue. Leaving the trio to their newfound family reverie, I slip a wineglass off a shelf, listen to the glug as I pour myself a glass of shiraz from the bottle Otto left open on the countertop, and sidle out of the room.

Cream

"Miraculous!" Otto says as we sit around the table. "That'd be the brand name." He swigs from his shiraz again and smacks his lips. "Think of the money you'd rake in?! Shampoo that makes you lose weight!" And he shakes his head at his own sheer genius.

It's dark now and crashing waves are raucous in the distance. The glass-topped table is strewn with the remains of dinner, gravied scraps of pumpkin and potatoes and carrots and green beans on dirty plates. None of the beef though, which, in the barbecue, shrank to the size of an embarrassed rabbit.

I look at Magda. She hasn't contributed a word to the conversation, eyes on her plate, knife and fork deliberate through her food, morsel by painful, deliberate morsel.

"There'd be a whole range, named after saints who've worked miracles: St Sebastian, St Perpetua, St Agnes –"

"St Vitus," Valerie butts in.

Otto won't be put off by her old joke. He sits back in his chair and pats his stomach. "Enough to build two places like this." And looking around the room, he beams.

"I always wanted a band. That was always a big plan, even as a kid. You know, goin' to gigs, makin' music." And knife and fork poised beside her plate, Valerie opens her eyes wide, like this is a huge revelation. And an incredible disappointment. And she nods.

Valerie is not the creative type. *Just add boiling water* is a stretch for her. So this is news. She spears the last potato on her plate, smothered in diet chunky rosemary and garlic gravy, and forks it into her mouth. She chews, while we all watch her, while we all wait. Then she says, still chewing, "Cnenhnee."

"I do not understand, Valerie," Magda says. Finally! Magda has broken her silence! I want to kiss Valerie for her attention-seeking behavior and lack of self-awareness.

Valerie leans back in her chair and pats her stomach. "That was going to be the name of the band," she says. "Cunt and Honey."

Kendalynn drops her eyes to her plate. Two marriages to Otto and countless hours spent with Valerie and her sister Trudy and still, Kendalynn flushes with embarrassment at Valerie's mouth. I catch a whiff of her sweet perfume.

"Is that Cunt '*n*' Honey?" Otto asks. "Or Cunt *and* Honey?" He peers at her, eyes squinting.

"Dunno," Valerie says. "Does it matter?"

"From a marketing angle, yes," Otto insists. His glass twirls between his fingers. "If you don't know what your product is, how can you promote it and maintain longevity?"

Otto doesn't usually talk like this any more, not since he sold his string of local hardware stores and retired to do the something he's still trying to find. In his sudden retirement – begun twelve months ago – he's had a lot of time to dismiss any idea that might take his mind off having too much free time. Now, his eyes twitch and his nostrils are dilating.

"Which one would you be, Valerie?" Magda asks. Placing her knife and fork together in the middle of her plate, the cutlery clinks with finality. "The honey, or the cunt?"

My brain flashes and I have to stop myself from thinking I'm in the audience of that 5.30pm TV game show and yelling, "The cunt! The cunt! Take the cunt!"

Valerie raises her eyebrows. "You need to ask?"

"Jesus, Valerie, it's always the cunt with you!" Otto is on his feet with lightning speed, chair smacking against the Lithuanian tiles as he stabs the air with his finger. "And you've been like that since you were twelve and it was Trudy's tenth birthday! Always the fuckin' same!"

Oh god, this is one of those Oedipal / Elektra moments I think, when … well, maybe the myths and legends are mixed up but still, it's sticky, and I was there at Trudy's tenth birthday party, twenty plus years ago …

... it was during Otto's first marriage to Kendalynn, when Kendalynn was still called Nancy. I was teaching high school English and History and living with a Croatian air hostess called Dubricza, when she was in town. She was tall and brunette and the first woman I ever knew who waxed everything, years before the Brazilian mass-market overkill. We were seeing Otto and Nancy / Kendalynn almost every weekend. And on an access visit Nancy / Kendalynn threw Trudy a slightly late tenth birthday party.

The usual kids' party food littered the table: fairy bread, the multi-coloured 100s and 1000s already leaching into the margarine; Jatz biscuits spread with butter, and cheese angled on top like sailboats; little frankfurters (aka little boys); lemonade that tasted only of sugar; and Nancy / Kendalynn had ordered a Dolly Varden cake: a doll with hair the colour of over-ripe straw stood in the middle of a cake made to look like an old-fashioned hoop dress, acres of pink mock cream in fake fabric folds and flower buds and ruffles on the outside, the cream covering the doll's breasts, her arms out-stretched as if desperate to be rescued from her cakey confinement.

Candles were lit and sung to and blown out and just as Nancy / Kendalynn had the knife poised to cut the cake, Otto ripped the doll out of the cake, pushed its arms above its head and sticking out his tongue, pink and writhing, licked the cream off its breasts.

There were dutiful laughs – someone even said "Ooh, saucy!" in a stuck-on British accent – but a stunned silence fell across the whole party when Valerie, twelve years old but tall for her age and older than she looked – perhaps it was her curly hair piled on top of her head – ripped the doll from Otto's hand and stuck her tongue between the doll's legs.

And pulling away, a cream moustache quivered on her top lip.

"I didn't even know I was a dyke then, I just wanted to piss you off!" Valerie says, standing across the table and looking Otto square in the eye. I read her t-shirt again and notice a misprint: it actually says *Dadd'ys Little Devil*. I guess no apostrophe's going to impress Otto at this point.

"It would be lovely to talk about something else," Kendalynn says, eyes moving from Otto to Valerie to Otto and back, "before the mood is completely ruined." She reaches across the table and starts stacking plates.

"What's for dessert?" Valerie asks, as she sits down, like she's recommencing the Last Supper. "Cake?"

Zapped! again

I hear the distant clinking of china and glass and Magda from the kitchen as Kendalynn asks, "What do you think about expanding into yellow?"

Kendalynn's sitting in one of the oversized white leather armchairs, a tray table in front of her, turning a pile of lace and pink fabric into a doll's dress. "Perhaps just purple is too limiting for the shop. Maybe just a corner of yellow." She snips a piece of lace with a large pair of lilac-handled scissors then rests the scissors in their special place on the tray table.

"If you're gonna call it *Rainbow*, you could have a corner each for all the colours of the rainbow," Valerie says, stretched out on her side on the overstuffed white leather four-seater sofa. Elbow bent and head cupped in her hand, a beer rests in front of her stomach. She flexes her toes and yawns. Suddenly she's the retail expert.

Kendalynn shakes her head. "But the shop is square so there are only four corners."

"But it's an old house, and Sappho Antiques uses more than one room. You could do the same. You could have a room for each colour." Valerie looks at me for confirmation. "Doesn't Sappho Antiques use more than one room of the house?"

Even swallowed by the white leather three-seater sofa I'm sitting in – counting all the seats in this room, there is space for fifteen to sit comfortably, in the sofas and armchairs alone – I am, of course, drawn in. It's conversational quicksand. "As a store room or a show room?"

"Both. Either. One can be converted to the other anyway. One woman's store room is another woman's show room."

"I didn't really count the rooms," I say. "It was stuffy in there and hard to concentrate."

"Hmmm, I don't know," Kendalynn says, rejoining the conversation. She places two pins between her lips and immediately takes them out again. "What do you think, Otto?"

Otto is crouched on the floor beside the widescreen television, fingering various buttons on the mock-titanium remote control and not getting anywhere. "Dunno," he says, not looking up, voice flat and determined to stay in his own world … or not enter theirs. "I gave up thinking when I retired."

The clinking china in the background has stopped. So this is my cue to wriggle forward out of the over-comfy sofa, place my bare feet on the cold floor, push out of the three-seater with gripping hands and clenched thighs, and return to the kitchen.

Magda had volunteered to do the dishes.

("We can just stack them in the dishwasher," Kendalynn said.

"I will do them," Magda said.

"I'll dry if you wash," I added.

"They are *my* dishes," Magda snapped, her knuckles white as she squeezed detergent into the banquet-sized sink.

I left her to it.)

But there's no sign of the dishes – they've all been washed, dried and put away. And there's no sign of Magda in the kitchen, just the smell of her signature too-much-dishwashing-detergent.

I stick my head inside the pantry and she's not tucked away there either, getting her fill of cardboard. I walk upstairs and she's not in the bedroom – I think of grabbing my jacket from on top of my backpack: it's night but the day was warm. Do I? Don't I? – nor is she in the bathroom, so soon I'm on the beach again. It's dark and waves hiss onto the sand. I spot Magda's white shorts in the distance. Despite the heat during the day, it's now too cold to run on the harder sand near the surf and risk getting my feet wet, so my bare feet slip on the softer sand and I take what seems like forever to reach her.

As I draw closer I hear her say "Zap! Zap!" in a loud voice, pointing the zapper at the sand and pressing the button. She stops and I stand right beside her but still she looks at the sand, zapping.

"Do you really think you're going to create glass sculptures with that zapper?" I say.

"Anything is better than this boredom," Magda says, zapping the sand again. "It is so bored here."

She twists the zapper in her hand and she is clearly not interested in talking to me – she's looking at her feet, at the sand, at the zapper – so I grab the zapper from her grasp and throw it away towards the water.

"It's *boring*, Magda," I say, as the zapper bounces on the compacted sand. "The word is *boring*. It's so *boring* here, that's what you mean. *Bored* for your own feelings, *boring* for the other person or object. *It* is boring. *You* are bored. *That's* the rule with adjectives in English. If it's not too *boring* for you to learn now."

Magda strides over to the zapper and picks it up. "You think I am a poor speaker of English also."

Running her hands over it, fingers caressing the shaft, she wipes the sand away.

I say nothing, just look at her.

"Thank you for your defending of me, Hugh." She flicks the zapper button on and off and on and off, hoping it still works.

Looking at her, I wonder what an observer would think, two adults on the beach at night, arguing while alternately tossing and fondling an electronic gadget. And I can't help it: I smile at the thought.

"You think I am as stupid as your friends think of me."

"They don't think you're stupid Magda, they just don't know why you ..." But I stop. Magda flicks the switch on the zapper and flicks it again and again but all we hear is the empty flick of the switch and the lack of an electric follow through and the frothing sea behind her.

And my breath, panting.

She drops the zapper on the sand and looks at me. It's too dark to see what her eyes are saying but her shorts glow white in the moonlight.

"They don't know why you mangle English when they know you lived in Ireland for a number of years, where you had to speak English every day ..." I fold my arms across my chest and stare at her, waiting for her reply. "They don't know why you play the crazy German woman with the zapper and the iron and the opinions."

"It is a culture difference." Magda crosses her arms across her chest, perhaps to stop from reaching out to me. Or maybe me reaching to her. "We are more honest and we *share* our thoughts and opinions." The breeze blows her blonde hair in her eyes but her arms are still welded across her chest. "We are not Anglo-Saxons."

"I don't know why you play the crazy German woman either," I say. "You had that 'phone call with Jörg and you've been in a bad mood ever since."

We're like two cowboys squaring off in the main street except it's windier and soggier and smells saltier.

"You test people all the time and then you wonder why they think you're strange," I add.

Magda bends down and picks up the zapper again. We could do this all night, I think, zapper and crossed arms and uncrossed arms. We made our points and now we're just circling.

"It is so boring here," she says again. She looks out to the sea, then back at her feet as she digs a big toe in the sand. "I want to go home."

"And where's that Magda?" And I know I've got her. "Where is *home?* 'Cause you never say *our place*, you always say *Hugh's house.* You said tonight, *I make pies always at Hugh's house.* It's never *our house*, it's always *Hugh's house.*"

She crosses her arms again, then flicking her big toe out of the sand, rocks on her heels. "It is not my house, Hugh. I have an apartment in Berlin."

I look up the beach. In the distance another couple walk towards us, holding hands. They could be us if we weren't so shitty with each other.

"And it is not your house either Hugh, it is your mother's house."

I smile and shake my head.

"There is nothing about you in *your house*," Magda continues. "It is all your mother's things and her furniture and you want maybe to leave so you do not make any changes in it. It is a nice house but it is not your house and it is one hundred percent not my house. It is a dead woman's house."

I look at my feet.

She's right. Nothing has changed except my mother is no longer living there. Magda makes it sound creepy. And it is.

"Maybe you make no changes because you do not really want to be there either."

And I know that yes, she's got me after all. Because really, I don't know where I want to be.

Lights Out

I went out with six girls in Uganda. I had a terrible time.

The sound of a car driving past surges through the open window, and I look up as headlights play on the bedroom wall. A breeze brushes the curtains – a faint smell of acrid car exhaust, no amount of money can stop that – and Magda shifts beside me. I feel her warmth move millimetres closer, though I'm not looking at her. No tilt of the chin down towards her. No flick of the eyes off to the right.

I look down again at the book.

I went out with six girls in Uganda. I had a terrible time. Michael was with me –

My eyes blur on the page and I yawn. My left shoulder aches too, with tension and not enough support. I'd get another pillow – there's a pile Magda placed on the ottoman in the corner near the window: Kendalynn favours the Turkish harem style of bedroom decoration, her talent for pastels enough to dull anyone's senses – but then I'd have to get off the bed and the mattress springs would squeak and I'd make my presence felt.

The only sound I can hear now – the ocean is silent in sympathy – is the tick tick ticking of my watch. Five past eleven.

I went out with six girls in Uganda. I had a terrible time. Michael was with me the whole …

I turn the pages, four more 'til the end of the chapter.

Magda's bra lies splayed on top of her backpack, airing. It's her only concession to anyone's comfort. It's a cliché, I know – yes yes yes, I get that it's a cliché! – but there's a Berlin Wall between us, marked by a lemon-coloured stripe on the quilt cover.

– six girls in Uganda –

We're both on top of the bed, it's warm in the room despite the frost between us – though maybe it's displaced energy – and we lie nonchalant but determined, pretending nothing is wrong but communicating little beyond hostility and disappointment.

– Uganda –

My fingers leaf through the pages and I count: 81, 89, 97, 101 – and I start again at the top of the first paragraph.

I found her brand of shampoo on the supermarket shelf.

I would close the book – the same airport novel Kendalynn lent me yesterday – but if I do, I have to concede to the tension crackling between us. Magda lies on her side, her thin frame barely denting the covers – okay, I'm stealing a glance at her now – facing away, the lamp her side of the bed throwing light across the planes of her cheek and illuminating her blonde hair.

I found her brand of shampoo on the supermarket shelf, green plastic –

Magda makes a noise, a deep breathing–snoring–snorting sort of sound and I breathe out, slow, silent, suspended.

I lay the novel on the chest of drawers beside me and look at the shadows the light makes on the folds of Magda's white shorts. She must be tired: normally she would take them off before lying down, so they're easier to iron in the morning.

A long, quiet hiss … and five seconds later, as the smell hangs putrid around me, I realise … Magda's farted.

Again, I'm in the firing line.

A silent intake of breath, through my mouth.

I wasn't aware farting in your sleep was possible until, newly-arrived in Berlin, I started seeing a woman from Belarus who ate a lot of eggs. After one particularly sulphurous night I stopped returning her calls.

Given the opportunity, I'm usually a sound sleeper. But the Belarusian woman and I … it was a new low in East – West relations.

Magda stirs, and she nuzzles her cheek further into her pillow. This time last night I was sliding in and out of her. Sometimes she gets so wet we make raspberries, a glopping suction sound with each withdrawal. And then a farting glomph when I push back in. Sometimes we laugh about it. Sometimes we ignore it. If she was naked I could lie behind her now, slide inside, slowly wake her up with the rhythm.

This – yes, I realise – is teenage fantasy. Or non-age-specific fantasy.

Ha! she would probably pretend to sleep through it anyway, she's so angry. And wake up in the morning saying she's had nightmares.

Magda says prune juice is what keeps her so lubricated but I'm sure it's mind control, some brain-to-vagina shortcut that gets things going. She could probably get work as an *After* model for vaginal dryness prevention crème.

Now – yes, I realise – I'm sounding like a daytime TV spruiker.

There is something entirely admirable about Magda's self-control. If anyone could ever regulate her vaginal secretions like a tap, it would be her. She makes her mind up and bang, off she gushes.

It's her decision, and hers alone.

I've seen photos of her as a kid growing up in Magdeburg – yes, she's Magda from Magdeburg, deep in the old East Germany – and she has the same look of purpose in her eyes even then as a ten-year-old member of the *Freie Deutsche Jugend*, the Free German Youth, staring out at the camera, eyes knowing and dissecting and adult. It's that old question: is she like she is because she's German, or is she like she is because she's like she is, or is she like she is because … ? Actually, it's an open-ended question.

I want to reach out, run my palm along the skin of her thigh, search up under her cuffs and deep into the crotch of her shorts, sink my pelvis against her arse, push her knees up under her stomach and crook my arm over her and draw her in to me.

Of course, there's the question of her white shorts getting in the way. And her underwear. And her resistance.

Ah, who knows when that will happen next anyway?

A big sigh from Magda – yes, it's a sigh, not a fart – and she reaches up under the lampshade and with a click, turns the light off.

Instant darkness.

"Hugh," Magda says, her voice cutting through the black. "I am moving back to Berlin."

Sunday

Communication is the key

"Oh, I like a nice crease in a pant." It's Kendalynn's voice, soft and knowing, in the hallway outside our bedroom. Probably doing her morning jog around the top floor.

"No," answers Magda, who's also in the hall. The door is open a sliver. But an important sliver. "Hugh thinks it makes me look weird by other people."

My eyes open. The view across my chest is blurry and bright. I dig the crust out of the corners of my eyes and flick it from under my fingernails.

Kendalynn laughs. "Oh, what do men know about fashion? You think Otto made all his money looking good?" She laughs again.

Silence from Magda.

"They just want clothes that are comfortable," Kendalynn adds. "They don't *care* how they look."

My gaze shifts to the door. Magda must have her hand on the handle, as the door is moving oh-so-slightly but there's no breeze.

"You want to iron your shorts every morning, Magda, you iron them. Don't let Hugh get away with being some kind of behaviour Na—" But Kendalynn cuts herself off before she finishes.

"No." It's Magda's voice again. "I need to go walking."

The door clicks shut. Their voices fade and disappear, and I'm left to contemplate the ceiling and the morning and the rest of my life.

I pull the sheet up under my chin – the doubled-over, double-sewn edge is still crisp in its new-guest-freshness – and listen to the waves folding onto the shore. And look at Magda's blue backpack against the wall by the ottoman under the window, and see she's taken the zapper with her. Maybe it's working again.

How could I have handled things differently last night, in the dark? It was very cut and dried, already decided, done and dusted and over and out. No correspondence will be entered into. Could I have thumped the mattress with my fist or pointed out the good things about life here – how she adores the weather, loves the ease of the city ... but how do you talk to someone who won't respond?

I could jump out of bed now and run off down the beach after Magda and her unironed shorts and dig my heels in and demand we talk about it but I'm sick of the sand, I'm starting to recognise individual grains and geology was never big on my list of 100 Subjects to Study Before I Die.

"I need to go back to Berlin and we never discussed how long you must be here to care for your mother. But now your mother has died and so now is the time for me to go," was all she would say – measured and even and determined – last night. I could tell she was shrugging, even in the dark. The mattress shrugged too.

"Can we talk about this?" I said, but how do you talk to someone who won't even look at you? (The lights were off but she was lying on her side and wouldn't budge. And leaping out of bed and moving around to her side and forcing her to look at my face as we spoke just seemed a little … youthful.)

I stare at the ceiling. How do you talk to someone who leaves the house before you've even had a chance to wake up properly?

It's a roll call of excuses, I know.

I snuggle down into the mattress and pull the sheet up under my nose.

The rich smell of bacon and eggs and sausages and tomatoes and onions and fried bread wafts up from the barbecue on the verandah and through the open bedroom window, a cruel and belated attempt at making this mausoleum cosy.

I close my eyes, and pull the sheet over my head.

Ming

It all starts with Kendalynn. "It's a lost art," she says. "It's really a dying craft."

Another time I would challenge her: is it dying or is it dead? Is it an art or is it a craft? Make a choice, Kendalynn! Of course there's geography and demography and ethnography to consider but my head is filled with departure dates and sands through the hourglass and lack of sleep so I sit on the loveseat in the corner, bare thighs cushioned on the red velvet and hang my head, staring at the Lithuanian floor tiles.

"We need to appreciate it while it lasts," she adds, "before it all disappears in a puff of smoke. And it's the last meal we'll have here this weekend, so let's do it right." And pulling out the coffin-sized drawer, she rifles through a stack of table linen until she reaches the bottom, and draws out a tablecloth.

"Oh, it's terribly creased," Kendalynn says, smoothing it with her hand. "Vanaemake used to dampen it and iron it flat on the table." She lifts the fabric to her nose and smells it, but I can't tell what she means to do: drape it across the tabletop, or put it back in the drawer, or throw it on the floor and perform some ancient ironing ritual like Vanaemake used to do or –

"Where's Magda when you need her?" Otto says, opening the back door to return to his barbecue, a large white ceramic serving dish in his hand. Breakfast smells waft in from outside. "Grub's almost up." He disappears again, the back door slamming behind him.

"Oh, Otto," Kendalynn sighs. In reaction to his jibe about Magda or his use of the word *grub* for food, who knows? And staring at the greying grout between the Lithuanian floor tiles, I think, who cares?

"Val–" she says, but stops. Stepping around the island cupboard, she mutters, "I'll do it," under her breath, and walks towards the table.

Kendalynn's grandmother – Vanaemake – was Estonian. Not a huge migrant group in Australia, and she was quite possibly the *first* Estonian woman ever to migrate to Australia – and maybe the last – and Kendalynn mentions her at the oddest times.

"Well, of course, my grandmother was Estonian," she said once, when we were buying loaves of bread at a continental bakery and she wanted the really dark bread. (*Dunkelbrot*, I think they call it, in Berlin.)

And Kendalynn loves opera too – the opera everyone knows, the opera anyone can sing along to because they use it in washing powder commercials on television – "Well, my grandmother used to go to the opera every week when she was a girl in Estonia" — which means precisely what? I can never work that out.

"I hope it doesn't have any holes in it," Kendalynn says, as she stands at the end of the table. The tablecloth falls out of her hands and unfolds onto the glass. "Silverfish *love* embroidery." Then she grabs two corners — lace is embroidered around the edge — and flicks the cloth out. It's gaudy — bright red tomatoes and glittery onions and lime-coloured artichokes and neon peas spewing down its length, but that's the fabric, not the embroidery — yet all that is forgotten when Valerie yells, "Look out for the vase!"

It's been left on the table, hopefully purple. And now we watch as it spins on its edge, flicked aside by Vanaemake's tablecloth, and teeters, and topples to the floor.

Crack!

No one moves. Kendalynn stands with her fingers clasping the corners of the tablecloth. Valerie leans forward and peers over the edge of the tabletop. And I sit in the loveseat, my open palms soft on the red velvet, and remember the vase had a chip in it anyway.

Valerie squats down and picks it up, her arse crack creeping above the waist of her jeans. Then stands up with a grunt and I see her t-shirt — has she slept in it? — has the word *Liver* in big black block letters splashed across it.

The vase is in two neat pieces. She holds one in each hand, like the Scales of Justice.

"Oh," is all Kendalynn can say. And in this morning light, as the sun streams through the kitchen window promising another beautiful day, the broken vase looks so *so* purple.

I hear a sigh. And it's coming from me.

"It's *not* an omen," says Kendalynn. "The shop will go on." She stands stock still, watching Valerie. Who, weighing each piece, looks like she's about to perform a juggling act with the vase halves.

"Yeah, two easy pieces," Valerie says, looking at her right hand and then her left. "Easy enough to stick back together."

"Do you have some glue in your car?"

Valerie shakes her head. "Don't think so. One hardware miracle a weekend is about as much as the ole Subaru can cough up."

Otto knocks on the back door with his elbow, so I stand up, walk across the floor, tiles cool on my feet, and open the door. I stand aside as Otto steps in with the ceramic dish piled high with breakfast. "Grub's up," he says.

"Oh, Otto," Kendalynn sighs. Again.

"Oh, Otto, what?" he snaps, kicking the door closed with his foot. "What have I done now?"

Kendalynn looks at the tablecloth, shakes her head and gathering it together, starts folding it. Maybe she's lost heart. Maybe she's decided we don't deserve it. "The vase is broken."

"It was a cheap piece of Chinese shit anyway," says Otto. Who built a hardware empire selling cheap pieces of Chinese shit. "Valerie'll have some glue in her shitbox."

"No, I don't," Valerie adds, "You'll have to go and buy some."

Otto places the ceramic dish (probably also made in China) on top of a thick Spanish cork trivet – it has *Made in Spain* stamped in the corner – on top of the kitchen bench. I see this as I've decided that, if I'm going to feel like shit, I may as well be eating while I'm feeling like shit. So I'm hovering at the bench, beside Otto.

(I don't trust those *Made in Spain* stamps. If it was really made in Spain, wouldn't it say so in Español?)

Serving tongs have been left on the bench, so I pick them up and dig into the steaming contents of the ceramic dish and – Otto is opening a can of beer at the sink ("Oh, Otto," Kendalynn says again. "It's *Sunday*, woman," Otto replies) – I pull aside two rashers of bacon, revealing the caramel brown of barbecued onion underneath.

I slide the top plate off the stack, china scraping against china, and piling my plate high with the sweet-smelling onion, it coils and slips across the white of the plate, and my mouth fills with saliva.

Valerie places the vase halves on top of the bench and stares at the mound I'm making.

I lick my lips and, grabbing a fork, retreat to the corner of the vast room and plonk myself in the loveseat, the red velvet plush against my thighs again.

"You like a bit of onion there, mate?" Valerie says, jaw clicking.

"Yeah," I say.

Three pairs of eyes stare at me, but fork twirling in the onion, I tuck in anyway, shovelling it into my mouth. If I'm going to confront Magda, I think –

The smooth caramelised taste lathers my tongue, followed by a smoky undertone. I swallow, thinking I should start writing restaurant reviews, maybe, and fork in another mouthful.

When she returns from the beach, I'll confront her, I think. And I can't do that on an empty stomach.

Penguin

"I just want to make some photos and then we can go back," Magda says, stepping onto the causeway. Her shoes, white and athletic, squeak as they hit the long, black rubber sheets nailed on the causeway between the tram rails. I step over horseshit fresh from the last horse-drawn tram ride, and breathe through my mouth so I can't smell the wet ripeness wafting up from the rubber. The horse tram is a holiday and weekend treat, the horseshit a tourist industry bio-product.

The sun glints off Magda's new ring, her left hand flashing with each swing, her Leica dangling from the string looped round her right. She is mistress of her own destiny, one foot in front of the other striding ahead. Or rather, is it me, hanging back, each step slower than the last, putting more distance between us? I squint, and see Magda's stride is more mad than machine, and her chin may be cocked but her pacing is off, lopsided and listing. She tosses her blonde hair in an open-air act of defiance, but I know she is uncomfortable in her unironed shorts, and smirk at her cheeky gait. While the luck of the ring has altered her mood a little, she'll be back to pissed-off and silent later.

*   *   *

An hour earlier Magda had walked into the dining cavern with her zapper in one hand and the ring in another. "I found this," she'd said, her hand open, the ring – gold, with a small diamond – sitting on her palm.

"Ooh, it's an omen," Kendalynn cooed, happy with the very thought that minutes earlier, with the cracked vase, she'd dismissed. She stood up from the dining table and picked the ring off Magda's hand, holding it up to the light.

"Some poor bugger's lost her ring, though," Valerie added, forking breakfast bacon into her mouth. And she laughed, her mouth open, pink meat and glistening fat roiling around as she chewed.

"A bit painful when you lose your ring," Otto added.

Valerie snorted. "Someone's out there now on ring patrol."

Kendalynn breathed out, squinting at the diamond. "It looks expensive."

"You'll have to give it back," I said, voice flat, the wowser in the corner, dirty plate on my lap. "You'll need to put an ad in the paper with a photo."

Now, I knew this was ridiculous. Unless there was some jewellery vigilante stalking the beach, searching out lost items and returning them to their relieved owners, the ring was lost to someone and a bonus to someone else. But this was too delicious to leave alone.

"It could be an heirloom," I added, knowing I sounded like a kid offering reasons for staying up past his bedtime. "It could be the key to someone's future."

"It looks too new to be an heirloom," Kendalynn said. "Maybe if you wear it on the main street in Victor Harbour and flash it about a bit, someone will recognise it."

I ran my finger around my plate collecting the onion juice, wet skin squeaking, then stuck the finger in my mouth. Magda hates it when I do that.

I watch Magda stop ahead. She looks through her camera, points the lens to the right and snaps a photo of the southern summer sea. The day is promising to be gorgeous again, with a light breeze playing off the sparkling water … but it's not the day to be out looking for postcard shots of fairy penguins. They come out at night, when it's cooler, to feast and play and waddle, but my face was a blank when Magda spoke of this. I want to see the disappointment in Magda's own face when, once we've circumnavigated Granite Island on its dusty walking track, she admits she hasn't found any penguins to happy snap.

I stop. My hands now on the wooden rail, smooth with the caresses of decades of South Coast visitors, I gaze out, back to the Norfolk Island pines lining the Victor Harbour esplanade with their tall shade and holiday silhouettes. They tower towards the clear blue sky and I wonder if those who planted them – aren't they another memorial to the fallen? – could have known how tall they would grow and how long they would stand.

I wonder about Valerie and Otto too, searching the Victor Harbour main street hardware store for ceramic glue to stick Kendalynn's dream back together.

A seagull cries above, off to the right, closer to Granite Island, down the causeway, but no, as its cries grow more insistent, it's not a seagull after all. I see Magda again, first hands on her hips, then arms flailing as she makes what looks like a desperate point.

A split second decision and I am walking, my own shoes, white and athletic, thumping and decisive on the black rubber, down the causeway, towards the commotion. I could just as easily turn in the other direction and hear about Magda's righteousness from the prophet's mouth later, after her possible arrest for assault and battery and arm-flailing, but something gets the better of me and as I draw near, I recognise the man she is speaking to.

I recognise the old faded red jacket from yesterday.

I recognise the sigh I hear coming from me.

Yesterday …

It was a different spot but it's the same man. And turning away from Magda, he whips his rod and line behind him and casts it out to sea.

Magda is screeching at the fisherman, her mouth a righteous wail. She stands between him and a baby capsule, the kind you use in your car facing the rear window. And facing me, away from the sun, there's a sleeping baby inside.

The man whips his fishing rod behind him again, then arcs it out over the water. The line whistles through the air and plink! plonks into the sea.

"You are going to spear your baby!" Magda booms.

He flicks a glance at us. But we could be on the moon.

"I will report you to the police," Magda adds, "and your name will be in the newspaper for a bad father!"

The man leans over the rail and with his fishing rod still clasped in his hand, spits into the water.

Three years ago: a classic Berlin moment. It was winter, and tired of waiting in seeping-to-the-marrow cold, I crossed the road while the red man – and not the permitting green man – shone across at me.

Silent street.

No cars.

When my feet touched the kerb on the other side, a woman admonished, *auf Deutsch*, "You're a bad man! You shouldn't cross the road like that! You're teaching children a bad lesson!" And she looked down at the sleeping child in the pusher in front of her.

I looked at the child, still asleep, and looked at the woman and looked down at my shoes – big black winter boots – and stepped off the kerb again and walked back across the road, the red man still shining at me. And turned and waved at her from the other side. And stood waiting, while the mother shook her head at me. Thirty seconds later I crossed again, the green man winking this time.

I grab Magda's elbow and pull her back along the causeway towards the beach. Her Leica bumps against her arm and her shoes slap against the black rubber. My heart thumps inside my chest.

"I am not someone how you can just take me, Hugh," she snaps. And she wrenches her arm from my grasp, standing stock still in the middle of the causeway.

My jaw sets in my chin and I glare.

"Your eyes are popping Hugh and it is very unattractive." Magda shifts her weight from hip to hip but her feet stay rooted to their spot.

But *my* feet won't stay still and they head for the shore.

Magda's feet are soon thumping behind me. "You know he is a bad man, Hugh." She breathes. "Why are you letting him do that?"

I want to sneak a look back at the fisherman – you can't fault Magda's logic, what she's saying is perfectly true – but her Berlinerin ballsiness has a time and a place.

"Why are you avoiding this issue?" She is beside me now, her words spitting on my shoulder, but still I charge ahead, feet slapping hard on the rubber. We are neck and neck, charging towards the shoreline, heavy breathing together, arms powering and legs grinding and minds matched.

I sneak a glance and catch the glint of her new ring on her finger.

"Watch out!" Magda says.

And just as I look down I step – splotch! – right in the middle of some horseshit.

"Oh, Hugh," Magda says. But she's not laughing.

With a sea view

"The fridge fuckin' stinks. Take everything out of the fridge and put it in the bin then put the bin out on the street. It's bin night tonight."

She drags on her cigarette and blows the smoke at the headstone beside the one she's sitting on. Then, mobile 'phone still stuck to her ear, flips the cigarette butt onto the gravesite and stamps it out with the toe of her purple plastic sandal.

A breeze blows up from the coast, dispersing the cigarette smoke – I can smell the salt on the air, and eucalyptus from the gum leaves too – but can't see the water because the gum trees block the view. If the residents were alive they'd complain about being ripped off.

"Yeah, yeah," the woman says, the most non-committal *yeah* I've heard all month, and scratches her head, peroxide ends fluttering as dark roots flatten open. And picking up her mottled brown handbag from its spot beside the headstone, vinyl fraying at the seams as it swings from its straps, she pulls out what looks like a mint and throws it into her mouth. But it catches and she starts to choke, the wheeze rattling in her throat.

We look at her, the two of us — Magda is sulking in the car, Valerie is striding to the top of the cemetery's boundary fence, up the hill — but make no move to help as she gasps and splutters and clutches at her throat.

Help her: we're abused. Not help her: we're abused. That's what I'm thinking. So we stand rooted to the spot, as solid as the gum trees dotted about us.

She breathes in again, a hacking rasp, then coughs into her hand. With a hack, the mint dislodges onto her palm and, wiping her eyes with the back of her other hand, the one holding the mobile, she throws the mint back into her mouth and she's back to sucking on it and spreading her view of the world.

"That was really nice," she says into her mobile. "Especially the second time."

She swivels on her headstone and turns her back to us — finally, I think — and snorts. "Who the fuck knows," she adds.

This spot is the final resting place of Otto's wife Brenda, the third one, the one he married between his bouts with Kendalynn. Who found a lump in her breast and six months later was gone.

I was overseas at the time — pre-Berlin, maybe in London or Italy or South America — and hardly knew her. Kendalynn came back into Otto's life and nursed Brenda in her final weeks. This might seem strange but you can't fault Kendalynn's generosity. Brenda was Kendalynn's sister, after all.

Keeping it in the family, Otto said, when I was back in Australia on holiday and learned he'd just married Brenda.

(He's never said it, but I think Brenda's the big love of his life, the one who got away.)

Next time I was back to Australia, he was marrying Kendalynn again. Who I still thought of as Nancy.

"We don't talk about it," Otto had said as we walked towards her grave, Otto's black rubber thongs and my own white shoes rustling the grass beneath our feet, "Kendalynn comes on her own sometimes."

He bends down and, crouching on his knees, reaches forward into the bricked-off garden bed and flicks eucalyptus bark away from the small upright plaque, throwing it behind him. Further uphill. Where the next breeze will probably just blow it back down again. But it's the thought that counts.

"*Brenda Mylene Otto, nee Laurits*," Otto reads aloud. "By the time she passed away the family situation was so fucked up, no one could agree on what to put on the plaque," he smiles. And then he sighs. "Ah, those *were* the days."

The woman in the purple plastic sandals slams the door of her car – some old rustbucket station wagon – but she's still talking on her mobile, nasal voice intruding on our day.

Otto claps his hands on his knees and pushes himself up. "Still, I've got the girls," he says, dusting off his hands. "You ever wanted kids?"

"Never really thought about it," I say. When really, the answer is, I never really *wanted* to think about it, and with a string of girlfriends and plans to move and a globetrotting career as an English as a Second Language teacher … well, it's wrong to talk about birth anyway when you're standing on a hillside surrounded by a celebration of death.

I look back at the car.

"Best thing to keep you young, kids," Otto adds. "You really miss out by not having 'em."

The dry bark and leaves crackle under his feet as he walks towards the car. I shake my head.

"What?" he says, stopping. He puts his hand in his shorts pocket and pulls out his keys.

I look him in the eye, a split second, then I look past him, up at the candle pines lining the narrow road. "Two days ago you said kids fuck you over and break your heart."

I've stopped shaking my head, so Otto starts shaking his.

"Nah, but that was Friday, mate," he says, his hand swatting a fly from his face.

We look up the hill. Breasts bobbing under her t-shirt – this one has *Chinese junk* written across the front – Valerie strides down the hill towards us.

"And a whole other era," he adds.

"Are we still going to the other hardware store?" Valerie says as she walks closer. "'Cause I really want to see the new development across the road."

Otto rolls his eyes. He points his keys towards the car and pressing a button, the car's lights flash. "Fuckin' greenies."

"Good," says Valerie, her stomping feet merciless on the dry leaves. "Glad you agree."

We pass the rustbucket station wagon as the purple-sandalled woman runs her fingers through her lifeless hair and flicks another cigarette butt out of her window. "If I can't sleep I just knock myself out with tranquilizers," she says. "And then if that doesn't work, I use a hammer."

Hardware

"Fuckin' greenies."

"Yeah?" says Valerie. "Well, it's fuckin' amazing."

I'm not sure if I should be impressed. It looks just like an ordinary upmarket subdivision to me, hulking designer houses side-by-side wall-to-wall, expensive façades fronting cheaper materials ever-cheaper the further you walk towards the back fenceline. (I see this from the side view of corner houses.) The faux lakes are a nice touch. Though they're ponds really, masquerading this late morning as drains as no water graces them beyond a brown sludge. And when the breeze changes direction, the stagnant pondweed smell hits at just the wrong angle.

"It's won prizes," Valerie says. "Big international ones."

Magda nods. She's not up to speaking yet, but a nod is a nod in the right direction.

"Probably designed by a whale-hugging lemon," Otto says, pointing his key towards his BMW, the lights flashing.

"Yes, whale-hugging lemons have all the best ideas." Valerie tugs her t-shirt down at the waist. The swampy breeze picks up and her nipples protrude through the thin fabric. She looks down and smiles.

The cypress trees we cruise past, lining the driveway and the car park, herald something great.

A palace?

A national monument?

A battlefield or ancient burial ground or scenic view out to the sea?

No, it's the hardware store, South Coast Building and Hardware, on the main road between Port Elliot and Victor Harbour.

"These trees are beautiful," says Magda as both car doors slam. She lifts her face to the sky and sniffs the air. "But they are nothing here. They should be lining the streets towards a palace."

I smile. Sometimes we are so in sync.

And then sigh.

"But it's a palace of dreams, Magda," Otto says, as the sliding doors sweep open and we step into the store, actually a huge shed or maybe even a leftover hangar bought cheap at an airport fire sale. "You can build whatever you like with anything from these shelves."

The ceiling is high, pitched into the ether, so in contrast, the shelves hug the cement floor. We fan out into the store, blending among the Sunday renovators dressed in plaster dust and paint swathes grasping colour charts and tape measures and stubby pencils in their grubby fists. Heads and shoulders are clear above the top shelves. Eyes lower, or fuzz if they stray eye-level: even in a hardware store on a late summer Sunday morning, it's rude to look like maybe you might perhaps appear to be sort of looking at someone.

Otto struts ahead, a king in his kingdom, except he abdicated and anyway, this hardware chain was never his to call his own.

"Shit displays," he says, a little too loud, turning and walking towards me, his rubber thongs slapping down the nail aisle. Or one of the nail aisles, I see, as I look over the top shelf and see more nails in the next aisle. And the next aisle after that.

Otto grabs a packet of large nails – BULK NAILS the packet says – and holds them out in his open hand. "Want a good nailing?" he says, looking at me like he's looking at a camera, misquoting himself from one of his TV ads from twenty years ago. When he was the king of hardware store self-promotion. Wearing his ole king of hardware sparkle, he could be twenty years younger. "Then South Coast Building and Hardware has the nailing you need!"

He tosses the packet back onto the shelf. "It's a fucking tragedy."

"What is?" Valerie's head pops above the top shelf in the aisle behind us. "What's he whining about now?" she asks me.

"That I had to sell the company because I didn't have anyone to take it over from me," Otto says.

"I'm just going to ignore that comment," Valerie says, "as the little man only wants another argument." And covering her mouth with her hand, she lets out a large fake yawn.

"Always the comedian," Otto adds. And looking away, anywhere but at Valerie, "I'm like a foreigner in my own country here," he says, and shakes his head.

"If anyone wants me," Valerie says over her shoulder, as she heads towards the large *Garden Centre* sign with the arrow pointing outside, "I'll be out on the terrace."

A thicket of lemon trees, all with tags fastened to their trunks. Some are planted in plastic pots and some in plastic bags and a few in wooden tubs. All are green and lush and leafy. Parting branches, Valerie emerges from the greenery, smiling.

"There's nothing happier than a happy lemon," she beams.

"Jesus!" Otto cries.

Valerie's hands fly to her hips, breasts jiggling under *Chinese junk.* "What, you're the only one allowed to make dumbfuck jokes?!"

Magda appears from behind Valerie. She hands me a label, unwound from one of the lemon trees, the twisty-tie hanging though the label's hole.

"You must buy this one Hugh, it is very draught-resistant."

I take the label and bite my tongue from correcting her. *Meyer*, the label says. When she knows Meyer lemons are not good in cheesecakes.

Is Magda still spoiling for a fight or should I step in and halt the bubbling argument between Valerie and Otto at the pass?

"But Meyers are not acidic enough for setting cheesecakes," I say. "And we've discussed this."

But Otto won't be silenced. "Is your sister *really* any happier being a muff-muncher?" he demands.

"Yes!" Valerie tosses her head. "Much happier!" And her breasts sway with bravado as jibes jab the air. "The happiest she's ever been. And she told you that herself, didn't she, and I was there when she told you."

Otto grabs a tag on the orange tree in a pot standing beside him and eyes down, pretends to read it.

"Didn't she, Dad?"

Otto thrusts his hands out in front of him, a final effort at explanation. "Ah, what does *happy* mean anyway? Fucked if I know."

"But you were yesterday not so happy with Trudy being a happy lesbian," says Magda, "Valerie. You said she was a big fat fake."

Magda takes the tag from my hand and disappears back into the lemon thicket.

Valerie's hands drop by her sides. "Well, that was yes-terday."

"It's her last husband I feel sorry for, the poor bugger," Otto says, hands on hips now. "Both his wives turning on him."

"It was gonna happen," says Valerie. "No one made Trudy run off with his first wife." Valerie sighs, and scratches her head. "It was just good luck and bad luck."

"Fuck bad luck," Otto sputters. "He should stop hanging around hockey clubs and start going to sewing circles."

Otto nods and I nod and Valerie might be nodding. And someone needs to say something.

"You know the best thing you can do for a lemon is piss on it," Valerie says. "They need the iron."

I see a flash of red in the distance, bolting away from us. "Hey!" I call out. The face of a teenage boy in a red South Coast Building and Hardware polo shirt turns his head. *Me?* it looks like he's saying.

The boy hesitates then walks towards us.

"Where do you keep your ceramic glue, mate?" Otto says. "We got a bit sidetracked here pissing on about the lemons."

Otto tosses the tube of ceramic glue over the roof of his BMW.

Valerie catches it. "Waddaya call a bunch of lemons?" she asks as she opens the passenger door.

No one answers.

As Magda and I settle into the back, Otto and Valerie's bottoms oomph onto premium interior leather and two car doors slam.

"A snatch," Valerie says.

I can't help it. I giggle.

The Apple of a Nun's Eye

"Oh dear," says Kendalynn from the front seat of Otto's BMW. She turns to us as we're folded in the back seat, her glasses perched on the end of her nose, hair framing her freckled face. "It says here, if we go on a Sunday they can't guarantee we'll be served by real nuns."

"But there's no time after today, we're going home," Otto says and then laughs from the driver's seat. "I want my nuns!"

Silence from everyone else.

Magda looks at me across our backpacks perched on the back seat, and raises her eyebrows. "So they are fake nuns on Sundays? Do they fake bless the food?"

So she's talking again. But is this a dig at country towns or Australia or Australian Sunday customs or Australian Sunday lunch customs or Otto and Kendalynn's idea of a fun Sunday pastime ... or at me? Those raised eyebrows aren't giving everything away.

Kendalynn, still twisting in her seat, looks down at the tourist booklet again. "It says the nuns lead a religious life and not all of them can work on a Sunday."

Kendalynn turns back to face the road undulating through the windscreen. I look out the side window at undulating vineyards.

"I hope we won't be disappointed," Kendalynn says. "It's good luck to see a nun on Sunday."

"Otto," Kendalynn says five minutes later, "does Valerie have her mobile? Maybe she knows another place we could have lunch."

Otto's BMW too small for five adults, Valerie is following behind in her Subaru. (Also, so she can leave when she wants, which may be sooner than anyone else thinks.) Looking through the rear window, I cannot see her car behind us. Is it too slow, or has it broken down?

"I told you," Otto says, his good mood infecting precisely no one. "I want my nuns!"

"Well, there might not be any nuns," Kendalynn snipes. "Which still doesn't answer my question."

But Otto is humming, just as he slows the car and turns onto a dirt road.

Two minutes later, we pull into an old schoolyard with a red brick building at one end and a fenced off area at the other. Looks like a playground with a solitary swing and metal stumps sticking out of the ground where once … what? … a slippery dip or climbing equipment or something else might have been? The stumps are like headstones in a dusty cemetery.

The derelict school was bought by a local convent, one we'd never heard of until Kendalynn found *St Jude's Jus* in the tourist booklet. Behind the restaurant – which still looks like an old country school – vineyards bask in the sun. I step out of the car, shade my eyes with my hand and look across to the double doors where a nun stands sentry to usher visitors inside. Except we are the only ones in the schoolyard car park.

Two car doors slam. "Well, we've seen our first nun," Kendalynn says.

"I think she must be a faker," says Magda. "She is too thin."

"Nuns!" Otto says, charging across the schoolyard like a greedy schoolboy in a sci-fi film.

The too-thin nun smiles a too-thin smile. "Welcome," she says, thin-lipped, and stepping out from the doorway, nods as we walk past her.

Inside, as our eyes focus in the dark – I think I see an altar that may double as the reception desk – "Never trust a hungry nun," Magda says.

I stand beside her, waiting for her next pearl of wisdom.

"But you will never know if she is really a faker," she adds, "until you push up her skirt and check her underwear."

Schokolade

"Are you American?"

"No," I said.

"Are you British?"

"No," I said.

Her brow furrowed. "You are not Irish?"

"No."

"Ah, my ex-husband was Irish, but you are not Irish?"

"No, not Irish. You forgot Canada."

She smiled. "Ah, so you are Canadian."

"No."

"New Zealand?"

"No."

Her eyes flitted across Friedrichstraße. "South Africa?"

I shook my head.

"So there is nothing left." She paused, open-mouthed. The Ampelmann turned green behind her and a group of shoppers stepped off the kerb and crossed the street.

"So you are really not American?"

I looked at her tanned jawline and blonde hair and hedged my bets and didn't turn down Französische Straße and disappear.

She smiled. "But your accent does not sound like an Australian accent."

"But it is," I said. "Just not the Australian accent you are used to."

She grinned, showing grey teeth, and the wrinkles around her eyes highlighted brilliant blue irises.

"I am going to Fassbender und Rausch," she said, brushing her hair from her face. "You must see their chocolate statues. You cannot eat them but you can watch them. It is a big place for tourists but for some Berliners also."

Lying naked in her old East Berlin apartment, I heard retching coming from behind the bathroom door. Or maybe they were sighs.

I knocked on the door. "Are you okay?" A streetlight beamed through the window. My penis cast a pendulous shadow across my thigh.

"Yes, I am just vomiting," she said. "Please make yourself at home."

Well, we *had* eaten a lot of chocolate at Fassbender und Rausch, I thought, sitting back down on the bed.

More retching.

Five minutes later she called me through the door. "Please leave your Handy number on the table, if you would like. The U-Bahn arrives every three minutes at Mohrenstraße."

I dressed, wrote my mobile number on the front of a Fassbender und Rausch menu, and shut the door behind me.

Shiraz

"Ugh, it was terrible." Magda swallows more wine. "He was a bad lover and he would not leave. I had to lock myself inside the bathroom and he still would not leave."

"Oh, it wasn't that bad," I say, looking at her, hoping she will catch my gaze and cease and desist.

The others at the table look down at their plates or finger their free-with-your-choice-of-wine glasses.

Magda is being the crazy foreign woman from Germany again. Maybe she *is* the crazy foreign woman from Germany. Maybe she can't help playing the crazy foreign woman from Germany because she's not *playing* her at all. She fidgets with the hair sitting on her shoulders, twisting it around her thumb and forefinger.

"So that is how I remember it, Hugh, and I have always a very good memory." Her jaw sets and her eyes glaze and there is no turning back. I look past her, through the large crucifix-shaped window and out to the sunny vineyard gracing the hill beyond and think about zoning out.

Otto coughs. Kendalynn wipes her mouth with her napkin. Valerie pushes her chair back and starts stacking our plates together. The noisy china cracks the air like a thunderbolt. Valerie wears her *Sound of Music* t-shirt, Julie Andrews dancing across her Alps.

"That is what I tell the people at my behaviour workshops. You must feel your mistakes before you can make them better." Magda picks up her glass again. "No, you must *own* your mistakes before you can make them better."

I look at Magda again, just to make sure she is not sharing a joke.

"Jeez, Magda," Otto's twang breaks in. "You really know how to bust a bloke's balls."

Valerie picks up the stack of plates and walks them to the service area. The coffee machine whirrs into cappuccino action behind the counter.

"But he is a much better lover now," Magda says, touching my arm. "You Australians do not like intimacy, you run away from it. But if you run too far you make a full circle and it comes back to eat you."

I look her straight in the eye. "I was never that bad," I say. "You were the first woman to lock herself in a bathroom over me."

Magda shrugs her shoulders. "It is good to be talking about this thing. So it is a good thing we did meet."

Valerie returns with the waitress. "Would anyone like to order dessert?" the waitress says, veil falling off her shoulder as she hands us each a dessert menu. She runs her hands down her front, smoothing her habit as she smiles and waits for a response.

We all — except Magda — bow our heads over our opened menus, and study the text hoping it will provide us with some salvation.

The nun-waitress clears her throat. "Reverend Mother's specials are chocolate pancakes with a shiraz and pineapple ganache," she recites, like she's working through the rosary, "Bartlett pears poached in shiraz, and a shiraz-infused gateau with grape custard served on shiraz vine leaves."

Magda snaps her menu closed. "Ah, maybe it was not you, Hugh," she says, placing the menu on the table, "but another Australian in Berlin I fucked."

Popular

"Fuck me, if this isn't God's country!" Otto says. He spreads his arms wide, welcoming the view and the sun and nature itself into his heart. "It's a bloody miracle, a minor fucking act of grace."

The view is, indeed, gorgeous, and looking west – I guess it's west, it must be west, though I'm too annoyed to check – I look past Otto and see gum trees in the distance and above that blue blue *blue* sky, no clouds, not even a puff, and the endless stretch of mid-afternoon.

I stop breathing and hear – I think I hear – the sound of my

own

heart

bea

ting.

I would spread my arms wide too, welcoming nature, but my arms are full, laden with four large jars of preserves, their lids topped with purple cloth covers: shiraz grapes in syrup, shiraz grape jelly, shiraz grape jam, shiraz grape sauce. ("Perfect for barbecues," the nun said as she deposited the sauce in my arms, though unable to tell if she was a real nun or not, I didn't know how much I could believe her.)

The sun is beating down on us I realise now, even through the cloth cap on my head, and the jars in my arms are heavy and and I wonder how long I can hold them before my hands give way and there's a shiraz explosion at my feet.

Kendalynn and Magda are still inside the school house, buying shiraz grape chutney and sun-dried shiraz grapes and shiraz grape tonic water as fast as the nuns can re-top each bottle and jar with purple cloth. (Kendalynn's attempts at wheeler-dealing with the nuns made me head for the fresh air – "Oh, I hope the shiraz grapes won't detract from the purple," she'd said.)

But it's Magda and her spoken-word memories of our first date that keep me stony-faced.

Otto holds an arm out, his hand floating in the air, like a leaf, I think, but actually it's mirroring the slope of the vineyard. The vine leaves, colours of rust and blood, shimmer in the sun. It's a perfect, gorgeous, sunny, Godly late late going-to-be-autumn-soon summer day when the chill of winter must be – *must be* – eons and eons away, and not a matter of mere weeks.

And then I hear the low hum of a plane.

Though it's not a plane, I realise as I look up, it's Otto, his hand coming in to land like a plane.

"Jeez," he says, and turns to me. His face lights up with a grin, probably because you could crack rocks on mine.

"I'd love to get my hands on this place and" – and here his fingers are clutching now, grasping in mid-air – "really turn it into *something*." He nods his head. Perhaps, in wonder. Or at the stupidity of those who could have built it into *something*, but haven't.

I turn away, to look at the old school house. Valerie stands on the other side of the car park / old schoolyard, talking into her mobile, kicking at the crumbling asphalt with her old sandshoe.

"This place has got a lot of potential, and you know …" and Otto swings around, arms open and signet rings glinting in the sun, to look at the whole 360 degree view, "… but I'm just looking to … I need to do *something*." And he nods his head again, and mutters, "I'm not dead yet."

I suddenly want to be inside the old school house too. Picking through the bottles and jars with spidery hand-written labels and dates and smeared-away dust as a nun gives a running commentary on their ingredients and cooking temperatures and sterilising processes and rubber rings.

I think that's what I want.

But my head snaps back. "Like what?" I ask, arms stretched and wrists aching, voice sharper than I'd like. Sharper than I'd like *maybe*. "What do you mean *something*? I thought you were retired anyway."

Otto shrugs his shoulders. And points to the vines on the surrounding hillsides. "Cabins," he says, "for weekend winemakers ... or a wine centre ... or you could clear out this central area here" – his hands are rotating in the air – "for a boating lake or ..." – and he shrugs again – "... or a rifle range."

I look back at the school house. I'm willing Magda or Kendalynn to step outside. And maybe Valerie to come over and tell Otto to shut the fuck up.

"A rifle range?!"

Otto looks straight at me. And out of the corner of my eye I see Valerie walking towards us. But the weekend is almost over and I am *done* with being the good guest who puts up with the host's dumb jokes and food choices and annoying personality and – now that I'm on a roll – why am I holding his wife's jars of preserves?

I pitch my voice louder. "A *rifle range?!*"

"Yeah," Otto challenges. "A gun club. Start it up and get some rich fucker from China to pay for it."

Denim on Valerie's thighs rustles up beside me.

"A fucking RIFLE RANGE?!" Valerie shouts. "Dad, haven't you made enough money?! How is it *possible* you need *more?* A rifle range?! With money from CHINA?!'"

I raise a very stern eyebrow at Valerie. I've had my voice taken away from me again and I wonder if, even with my arms filled with glass jars, I cast a shadow with these people.

"I'm a populist!" Otto says. "This place deserves more *people* coming here and appreciating it. I like to share things! God knows, I've shared enough things in my time."

"I *never* thought I'd hear you talking about getting into bed with the Chinese," Valerie says.

"You really mean a rifle range?!" I add, not giving up on making a mark. "You really think you can just come in here and buy up anything you want and build anything you want and charge any price you want and people will be kind to your memory?"

All the anger and the anger and even more of the anger stopped up inside me surges out of my mouth.

"Why not a paper mill?" I continue, the words vaulting out of me, "or a nuclear power plant?!"

But I can't throw my arms out and clench my fists with these glass jars weighing me down and I can't even get a chestful of air with these glass jars pressing against me either. Despite all my anger my voice is still too thin. I want it to roar over the vines but it flops and sputters somewhere on the asphalt.

"Jesus!" Otto says, his face red, a vein big and throbbing at his temple. "It was a JOKE!"

"But Dad," Valerie says, wrapping her lips around each and e-ve-ry syllable, "your jokes have a habit of turning into reality. You'd really want a business partner from China?!"

"Who the fuck do you think *bought* the hardware business?!"

Valerie steps back. "You sold that whole chain of hardware stores to someone from China?"

She cocks her head, like the words can't quite settle in her brain.

"No," Otto says. "Not from China. But that's the most interest you've *ever* shown in the hardware business. Ever!"

Valerie cocks her head to the other side and shrugs her shoulders. "You never wanted me to have it anyway."

I breathe in and look from one to the other, from Otto to Valerie and then from Valerie to Otto.

"Or Trudy, for that matter," Valerie adds. "Or even her kids."

Otto's head is down, looking at his feet.

Valerie's head is down now too, looking at her feet.

I breathe out. Because it's hot standing on the asphalt in the middle of this family showdown and I can't see *my* feet because of the glass jars in my arms, so I look at Otto again.

Otto snaps his head up, his eyes worried, maybe even cross-eyed, maybe because of the heat.

"And where's your sense of humour, mate?" he says straight at me, thumb jabbing. "It's like I don't even know you any more. How long have we been mates? Thirty years – thirty-five years – nearly *forty years!* And all weekend you've just sat back and judged."

Where did this come from?

"No, I haven't," I say.

"I know a fucking sneer when I see one," Otto says. "You don't need to say anything. You shit on my ideas but you're more than happy to sponge off the money I made from them."

God, we've got another hour and a half in the car on the drive home but I just want the day over with. This life, the one I'm in now, I think I want that over with too. And I definitely want these glass jars in my arms over with. And Otto's face is glowing – no *glowering* – red, just like the vine leaves looking so beautiful as they shimmer in the sun.

"Look mate," Otto adds, like he's offering condolences. "I'm sorry Magda busted your balls in there, if you're still pissed off about that. And who wouldn't be?"

My head shakes from side to side.

"But making money's what I'm good at," he says, his thumb now jabbing his chest. "It's the only thing I can really do." He lets out a breath. "That and piss people off."

"There are more important things than making money, Dad."

Otto whirls around to face his daughter. "And you've enjoyed the money I've made, too," he snarls. "It paid for your *private* girls' school and those *six years* at university so you can work at that women's refuge and for those *stupid* fucking t-shirts you wear."

"Someone had to spend it on something worthwhile," she laughs.

"It's a waste of ..." Otto starts, but then throws his hands in the air again. He looks at me, like he *really* wants to tell me something. His small, incisive teeth bite his bottom lip. Then feet stomping on the asphalt, he strides toward the BMW. And wrenching the door open as we watch, while jars clink in my arms, he shouts, "You've been too long away from Australia, son! You don't know where your *heart* is any more!"

And Otto throws himself into the driver's seat and slams the red door SHUT.

We wait, the two of us, Valerie and I, on the schoolyard asphalt. Otto's head bobs and his shoulders move and Valerie must hear the dull roar from inside the car because I can too, but other than that, while we're standing around wondering what to do next, all Otto's doing is a lot of yelling and sitting.

Jars clink in my arms again.

Vine leaves rustle in the breeze.

Sun's rays beat down.

Valerie coughs. "Gee," she says, and sighs. "Must be his time of the month."

Then she draws her foot back and kicks a stone clear across the schoolyard. It dings against the hubcap of Otto's BMW, and scutters across the asphalt.

"Oh well," she says, voice bright, "I'm off. My work here is done."

Feet scuff on the asphalt. A car door creaks open and creaks shut and her Subaru rattles into action and tyres flay on the ground and I think, yeah, Otto's right: that car really is a shitbox, but I see none of it, as I waddle off toward the horizon, clink, clink, and placing the jars on the baking ground at my feet, hands on hips, I look out at the blue blue *blue* sky and stand among the vines and breathe.

Deep.

Favour

The window buzzes down and Kendalynn sticks her head out into the late afternoon shade. "Anything within reason," she says. "You know, that you think people might buy."

Otto slams the fuel tank flap shut but his response is drowned out by the squealing brakes of a truck pulling in.

"What?" Kendalynn says.

Sitting in the back seat, I look around Kendalynn's headrest to see what's going on.

Otto's stomach and crotch appear level with Kendalynn's open window.

"It's research," Kendalynn says, "just make a note of the sort of things they're selling in purple." And then, "Hey, hang on," she adds.

Otto waits while she opens her handbag and rifles through it, pulling out a purple pen and a pad of pale purple sticky notes. Which she hands to him through the open window.

"Just write them down," she says, "it won't take long."

"I'm sure as hell *not* using a fuckin' purple pen and purple paper," Otto says through the window, tossing the paper and pen onto the floor at Kendalynn's feet. "Jesus, woman."

Magda sighs from her corner – she's spending all her energy looking everywhere but at me – while Kendalynn rifles through her bag some more, this time producing a yellow pen (with more acceptable ink, I assume) and an old envelope, which she hands to her husband.

Who says nothing, and disappears, walking across the dark grey cement and into the service station shop, to pay for the petrol and collate a list of purple products for his wife.

Kendalynn bends forward with a grunt and picks up the purple pen and paper from the floor, drops them back in her handbag, and snaps the clasp shut.

I sink back against the headrest and close my eyes. Hands resting by my side, my chest rises and falls. And rises. And falls. I'm half-asleep already, and hear a sort-of half-mumble behind my breathing.

"Hugh?"

Something half-nudges my leg and I open my eyes.

Magda's hand pulls away with a glint. She's still wearing the ring she found on the beach. "Kendalynn is speaking with you."

Kendalynn's body twists in her seat and her head is turned towards me. "I know you don't think much of my exclusive boutique-cum-general store idea," she says. She rests her chin on the side of the backrest. There's a smile plastered across her mouth.

"No," I say, before I realise I've even said it, my eyes half-open. And I shift on the seat. "No, it's probably –"

"But it'll give Otto something to do," she cuts in. Her glasses rest on the end of her nose and her freckles dare me to disagree. "He'll step in before the shop opens and we'll turn it into a café, maybe with a barbecue courtyard out the back. Just on weekends." She turns to face the front windscreen again. "So it won't be the disaster everyone thinks it will be. Maybe we'll continue with the purple theme, I like the idea of a purple café." She turns to look out the passenger window, and plays with the pink ruby and diamond rings on her fingers. "Purple is the national colour of Estonia, it was Vanaemake's favourite colour."

I catch Magda raising an eyebrow.

Kendalynn chuckles. "But he's not dead yet, and someone's got to spend some of that money he got when he sold his hardware empire."

"Yes," I say, though my mind is really somewhere else.

Kendalynn turns around to look at me again.

"But he's not coming around as quick as I thought he would to the idea of starting a new business." She smiles. "So maybe you could convince him it's a good idea?"

I'm brought back to the interior of the red BMW with a thud. What I know about business you could write on a business card.

"He always values your opinion."

Magda snorts. "But Hugh, he does not know anything about business."

"Sure," I tell Kendalynn. "I'd be glad to help."

I look at Magda but her eyes are closed. She lets out a long, low, deep breath.

Turning my face to the window, I sink back against the headrest, and close my eyes again.

Destination

"Thank you for driving us, Otto," says Magda, light blue eyes earnest in her tanned face. "The environment will thank you, too."

I step backwards onto the kerb as Kendalynn sits down on the passenger seat, swivels her legs inside the car and pulls the door shut. Then buzzes the window down.

"We'll have you over for dinner soon," she says.

"Sure," I say, and then without thinking, "thanks for a nice weekend."

Her goodbyes already over, Madga — zapper sticking out of the top of her backpack, clanking against her iron — walks up the short driveway towards the front door.

"Maybe next weekend," Kendalynn adds, hopeful. "If you're free." And then she says, a strain behind her smile, "Soon."

The engine revs under Otto's foot and I smell that most rarified of things, BMW exhaust.

"I'll email you," she says.

Kendalynn has never emailed me ever.

"I'll get your address from Otto."

The engine roars some more and the car pulls out into the street. "Thank Magda for the scarf," Kendalynn says, her head poking through the open window. "And tell her I really *am* interested in buying that ring she found." And rounding the corner, her hand waving, they're gone.

"Hugh, you have the key," Magda calls out.

The garden in front of the house is filled with Black Boy roses, their flowers a velvety red, six bushes, planted by my father years ago and then tended by my mother for years too. The bushes are gnarled, the branches knotty but cut them back hard – Queen's Birthday holiday weekend, early June, is best, Mum always said – they'll flourish in spring and through the whole summer.

"I like them because they have a meaning to you, Hugh," Magda said soon after she first saw them, "but all roses are ugly, I think."

She didn't mean just the bushes, but the flowers too.

Magda, backpack still slung over her shoulder, walks through the gate at the side of the house, no doubt to find the spare key hidden under the upturned pot under the old metal bucket beneath the old rainwater tank … where it's lived for at least thirty years. Not waiting for me with the other key.

I really should get out into the garden, the hibiscus bushes along the driveway – planted by me years after the roses, in a later attempt (my mother's instigation) at a hassle-free garden – need pruning too.

A car drives past – it's the men from three houses down, the heart specialist and the gynaecologist – and I wave, big arcs of neighbourliness. So big I almost sprain my shoulder.

They wave back, though the gynaecologist – he's in the passenger seat – grimaces in alarm at my semaphore.

A light flicks on inside and through the curtained front window I see Magda walking through the house, checking.

I should go inside.

A breeze rustles up and brown leaves from the gum tree next door blow into the front garden and settle among the rose bushes.

I should go inside.

I pick my backpack up from the kerb and sling it over my shoulder. Pushing my hand in my shorts pocket, my fingers find the door key.

I should go inside.

If I prune the rose bushes on the Queen's Birthday weekend, just at the end of autumn, as the weather really starts to turn, that's not such a bad time to be leaving, I think. Summer will be around the corner in Berlin and people will already be eating outside on the footpaths and in the beer gardens and along the canals and there's only twelve months left of my contract so it doesn't matter if I cut it a bit short.

Stepping up on to the front verandah, I slide the key in the lock, twist it, and nudging my shoulder against the front door, push it open.

Acknowledgements

Sent via email, March 2012

Hi – I need to get my own writing back on track and so I am enlisting your help!

My plan is to write a number of short stories based on themes provided by others. Think of it as cross-promotion!

The stories will be 250 to 500 words long, and credit where credit is due, a short 50 word bio of you as a theme-contributor will feature with the story.

Of course, the stories will be mine – I plan to make it available in print – and so I just need a prompt from you.

Dunno how many I will go for but I think there will be interconnected characters and stories.

And all you have to do is provide a prompt.

Thanks,

Matt

Thanks

Thanks go to the following writers who responded when I sent the original email asking for writing prompts in March 2012 (see opposite).

Those who provided prompts that were used include: Matthew Brennan (have all the stories set at an Australian vineyard); Rebecca Chekouras (nozzles, hoses); Michelle Elvy (after the deluge); Luisa Brenta (clash of accents among English speakers from different English-speaking countries ... and of course, Australians abroad); Berit Ellingsen (The empire thanks you! I sometimes say this to people I know well); Cheryl Anne Gardner (ugly play-ground); Gill Hoffs (glass. Can mean: the hard substance made of heated sand); Abha Iyengar ("I did not care for Sybil's forgiveness. I had to do this now. Or I would not be able to forgive myself."); Maree Kimberley (a middle aged mother and a young man meet outside a jail and have a discussion about the place of the roast dinner in family life); Len Kuntz (a strange man knocks on your door claiming to know you, and creepy dolls that take on the narrator's likeness); Maude Larke (miraculous); Meg Tuite (a conversation after awkward sex with a guy you just met and are trying to get rid of); and Stephen V. Ramey (what you see is what you get).

Thanks also to those whose prompts I used, and who are not holding me to the promise of *a 50 word bio!*

Some sent prompts that did not fit into the evolving story. So thanks also go to Nancy Chapple, Gay Degani, Jen Knox, Todd McKie, Linda Simoni-Wastila, Michael Webb and Nathaniel Tower.

And a very special thank you to Gill Hoffs, who back in the day, when these characters and their story first started burning brightly on the South Coast firmament, gave me a lot of useful feedback.

About the Author

Matt Potter lives in Adelaide, South Australia. He has, at times, worked as a social worker, usually in community services, but he has also worked (more enjoyably) as an ESL (English as a Second Language) teacher, in Germany and in Australia.

His books include *Hamburgers and Berliners and other courses in between* (travel memoir), *Based on True Stories* (short stories), *Vestal Aversion* (short stories and short non-fiction), and *all you need is ... a whiteboard, a marker and this book #1* and *#2* (ESL teaching resources).

Matt also moonlights as an editor, publisher, designer, lecturer, teacher, smalltime troubleshooter in the world of independent book publishing, and gardener. If you wish to hire him for his considerable skills as editor, publisher and designer, visit https://mattpottereditor.com/.

Also from TRUTH SERUM PRESS and PURE SLUSH BOOKS

http://truthserumpress.net/catalogue/

- *Kiss Kiss* by Paul Beckman
  978-1-925536-21-8 (paperback) 978-1-925536-22-5 (eBook)
- *Track Tales* by Mercedes Webb-Pullman
  978-1-925536-35-5 (paperback) 978-1-925536-36-2 (eBook)
- *Inklings* by Irene Buckler
  978-1-925536-41-6 (paperback) 978-1-925536-42-3 (eBook)

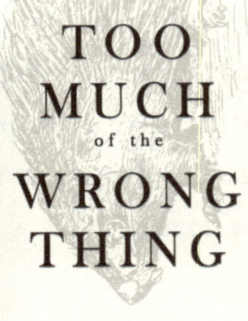

- *Happy² Pure Slush Vol. 15*
  978-1-925536-39-3 (paperback) 978-1-925536-40-9 (eBook)
- *Lust 7 Deadly Sins Vol. 1*
  978-1-925536-47-8 (paperback) 978-1-925536-48-5 (eBook)
- *Too Much of the Wrong Thing* by Claire Hopple
  978-1-925536-33-1 (paperback) 978-1-925536-34-8 (eBook)

Also from TRUTH SERUM PRESS and EVERYTIME PRESS

http://truthserumpress.net/catalogue/

- *All Roads Lead from Massilia* by Philip Kobylarz
  978-1-925536-27-0 (paperback) 978-1-925536-28-7 (eBook)
- *Wiser Truth Serum Vol. #2*
  978-1-925536-31-7 (paperback) 978-1-925536-32-4 (eBook)
- *True Truth Serum Vol. #1*
  978-1-925536-29-4 (paperback) 978-1-925536-30-0 (eBook)

- *Hello Berlin!* by Jason S. Andrews
  978-1-925536-11-9 (paperback) 978-1-925536-12-6 (eBook)
- *Deer Michigan* by Jack C. Buck
  978-1-925536-25-6 (paperback) 978-1-925536-26-3 (eBook)
- *Rain Check* by Levi Andrew Noe
  978-1-925536-09-6 (paperback) 978-1-925536-10-2 (eBook)

Also from TRUTH SERUM PRESS

http://truthserumpress.net/catalogue/

- *Luck and Other Truths* by Richard Mark Glover
  978-1-925101-77-5 (paperback) 978-1-925536-04-1 (eBook)
- *happyme@t.us* by Kim Conklin
  978-1-925536-07-2 (paperback) 978-1-925536-08-9 (eBook)
- *What Came Before* by Gay Degani
  978-1-925536-05-8 (paperback) 978-1-925536-06-5 (eBook)

- *Based on True Stories* by Matt Potter
  978-1-925101-75-1 (paperback) 978-1-925101-76-8 (eBook)
- *The Miracle of Small Things* by Guilie Castillo Oriard
  978-1-925101-73-7 (paperback) 978-1-925101-74-4 (eBook)
- *La Ronde* by Townsend Walker
  978-1-925101-64-5 (paperback) 978-1-925101-65-2 (eBook)